HIDDEN WORLDS
VOLUME 2

Jeffrey Peter Clarke

HIDDEN WORLDS
VOLUME 2

Imhotep

The day of his arrival found Stacey prowling one of the most important sites in all Egypt – the third dynasty step pyramid complex of King Djoser at Saqqara. His foray into an area where archaeological exploration was a never-ending task ought to conjure up something of interest for his readers. Would a mass grave speak of ritual slaughter? Did these people possess dark powers since lost to the world? Would beings from another planet have somewhere left their mark? He expected his readers, the gullible and the credulous, would be out there drooling.

Mike Stacey had freewheeled about Egypt and parts of the Middle East for years. From the solitude of numerous back-street hotels he had reported to the popular media on the real and imagined mysteries of the ancient world. He recognised no dividing line between the two, but hard facts were not what his readers craved. Had the over-publicised 'Curse of the Pharaohs' not already been established in the public mind, dapper, hawk-faced Stacey would have invented it. His earlier offering entitled, *Was Pharaoh an alien?* made no impression on the responsible media but had notched up a profitable airing where this brand of sensationalism held greater appeal.

Camera swinging from his shoulder, Stacey had infiltrated a group of tourists and their English-speaking guide where they gathered in raw heat beneath a cloudless, late morning sky.

'So as we stand before it,' announced their guide, adjusting mirrored sunglasses whilst his party gazed dutifully up at the decaying structure that had basked through some forty seven centuries, 'I can tell you that the great stepped pyramid and the part-restored walls and buildings we see all about us represent the first large-scale stone architecture anywhere in the ancient world.'

They gazed about, hands raised to shade their eyes. One slouch-hatted man, wiping the sweat from his forehead, said, 'You mentioned the guy who designed it all – this, er -.'

'Imhotep,' smiled the guide. 'Yes, he was the king's chief minister. He was a very important man with titles of his own.'

'Yeah, Imhotep – that's the guy. You said he was more or less as famous as the old king himself - so what do we know about him?'

'An interesting question,' replied the guide, 'but sadly we have no more knowledge of Imhotep than we do of the pharaoh. And famous as Imhotep was in his own day, he became even more so throughout Egypt as time went by – a legend, in fact. He was credited with supernatural powers. Two thousand years later he was worshipped as a god of wisdom, writing and healing. The classical Greeks identified him with Asklepios, their own god of healing and medicine. Imhotep may be forgotten now but for over two and a half millennia he was one of the most revered men in ancient Egypt.'

'Do we know,' asked a woman, fanning her face with a guidebook, 'what happened to him or where he's buried?'

'We've seen a good few pyramids and tombs on this tour,' added the first man, 'but nobody mentioned his.'

Stacey listened hard. Could this be an opening?

'You would think,' replied the guide, 'such a clever and resourceful man would ensure his own preservation after death but his final resting place has never been found. A British Egyptologist, Walter Emery, searched this area from 1964 until his death in 1971. He always maintained Imhotep's tomb must be somewhere hereabouts but he never did find it. They are still looking. In fact there's an important dig not far from here. So who knows? Maybe one day -.'

For Stacey the headlines were already flashing: *'Will Dead Magician Reveal Ancient Secrets?'*

***

Two fans creaked lazily above their heads as they sat around the table. Beyond the window, silhouetted against a darkening sky, arose the great step pyramid of a once great king.

'We've reason to believe,' announced stocky, round-faced Don McKenzie, head of the archaeological team, 'that another tomb lies to the south-west of Djoser's complex. It's concealed deep beneath the remaining northward extension of another complex, that of Djoser's successor, Sekhemkhet.'

'And what do we know about him?' asked Stacey who, after considerable pleading had been allowed access to an on-site office meeting that consisted of three members of McKenzie's team and two officials from the Supreme Council of Antiquities based in Cairo. Maybe they wouldn't reveal anything of world-shattering importance but Stacey was not one to dismiss routine matters when they might conceal the pearl of a revelation. The two smartly dressed officials were out of place, the air within the cluttered office was charged with unspoken words.

'Not a lot,' replied McKenzie, all too familiar with Stacey's disdain of professional values. 'Sekhemkhet had big ideas but only reigned as pharaoh for six or seven years and we've no clue as to where he ended up. His pyramid complex was intended to outdo that of Djoser but it never got completed. It looks to have been designed by the same architect since Imhotep's name was found on the north enclosure wall. Like Djoser's monument, it contained a large number of subterranean storage magazines: over a hundred and thirty in fact, as well as several galleries and the burial chamber. All of 'em were empty, including the alabaster sarcophagus, though oddly, the seals were still intact. So there's something for you to elaborate on, Mr Stacey.' A grin spread across McKenzie's face. 'Maybe the poor bugger got himself abducted!'

'So this new tomb,' queried Stacey, outwardly ignoring the abduction remark, 'could it be where they placed him – a kind of quick and easy solution before the next guy stepped in to take over?'

McKenzie hard-eyed him then replied, 'As I said, we don't know at this point who the tomb, if that's what it is, might belong to. It's possibly a relative of Sekhemkhet and it's probably long since been looted. That's all we can tell you at present, Mr Stacey.' Gesturing at the door he added, 'Now if you'll excuse us, matey, we have tomorrow's work schedule to discuss.'

They watched in silence as Stacey scraped back his chair, got up and walked to the door.

McKenzie waited long seconds after the door had closed then remarked to the officials, 'The less anyone says to that bloke the better. Now he's out of the way I'll update our progress. We've cleared all remaining infill material and reached the bottom of the shaft. The walls are roughly dressed all the way down. The shaft is little over two metres square and getting on for fifty metres deep. That's a lot deeper than the shafts beneath Djoser's pyramid or Sekhemkhet's might-have-been. We recovered a number of votary objects from the loose material and as you're aware, these have been recorded and delivered to the Cairo Museum. As we reported early last week, the remaining three metres of infill consisted of squared blocks of solid stone.'

He glanced at the door in case Stacey still loitered, then continued. 'The top layer was intended to look like a paved floor - as if this was a dead end and the work never completed. In one wall they'd carved out a false door with the name of Sekhemkhet above it. Opposite this a horizontal gallery had been started then abandoned by the builders after less than a couple of metres progress. If we'd not made last minute soundings in that floor we'd have fallen for the trick and sealed the shaft off as a dead end. It wasn't until this afternoon we managed to hoist out the last of those blocks and take a proper look down there. Our friend Stacey was hovering nearby pretending to be a tourist. We usually keep the likes of him away from working sites but at that point we didn't think we had much.'

'But now you do,' said one of the officials. 'Is what you have found of some importance?'

'Once the shaft was cleared,' McKenzie continued, 'two of us were lowered all the way down to the solid rock base. We discovered a bricked-up recess in the south side that had been disguised with grey plaster. We proceeded to clear this, sent up the rubble but left the bricks stacked against an adjacent wall to serve as a bench. Behind those bricks there's a wooden door. We're certain it conceals a passage or a chamber.' McKenzie opened the laptop computer. 'On the door is an unbroken clay seal bearing hieroglyphs. Here's what we photographed.'

***

'Those guys in suits weren't around for small talk,' muttered Stacey lighting a cigarette. He blew smoke into the warm night air then, perched on the remains of an ancient limestone wall, continued to observe the site office. 'There's something big going on. The amount of stuff they pulled out of that shaft, and those stone blocks – this one I'll be sticking with!' Before the cigarette was finished he was retracing his footsteps back to the cabin.

***

The screen lit up. McKenzie stabbed keys and an image appeared.

'Ah, I see it clearly,' remarked the first official as both peered closer to the screen.

'Yes,' said the other, 'it is obviously the owner's name but what does it say?'

'Imhotep,' replied McKenzie, casually. Then he hesitated to observe their expressions. 'We believe this could be his burial place. It may extend beneath the pyramid site of Sekhemkhet. It might have been planned that way even before work on the king's complex was started.'

'Imhotep,' breathed the second official. 'So - a tomb beneath a tomb - and it could be his.'

'It could,' confirmed McKenzie, 'and we must consider the possibility that it is intact. The Director of Antiquities should be informed soon as possible.'

'If this is the tomb of Imhotep,' declared the first official, raising his hands, 'it will be the find of the century. Yes, we will inform Dr Fergani at once. This site must be subject to the very highest security. It must be strictly out of bounds to all except those directly involved in the work of excavation. We will have no press or media of any kind there until the Director himself permits it.'

'That's what I like to hear,' responded McKenzie, 'especially with Mike Stacey sniffing about. This could be a more important find than King Tut and if the media get onto it we'll have 'em pouring in by the cartload. On the other hand if it proves to be empty then they'll be more than happy to lay on the ridicule.'

The computer was visible from outside one of the cabin windows. They were unaware of eyes studying the image on the screen. Unaware, too, of the camera recording it.

***

In the subdued light of the hotel room the screen glowed. A volume on Egyptology lay illuminated by a small lamp on Stacey's desk.

'Jesus Christ,' he breathed, 'if they've found what I think they've found then -.' He switched off the computer, pushed aside the book and stepped over to the window where he had a view of the city's lights and chaotic traffic.

Early the following morning he returned to Saqqara with a busload of tourists. Through binoculars he studied the posts and wire netting in the process of erection under the watchful presence of two police guards. Inside the enclosure stood McKenzie with two of his assistants, all wearing hardhats. Next to a gleaming black limousine stood a group of five smartly suited Egyptian officials.

Stacey watched them lower one of the archaeologists together with some equipment down into the shaft. A half hour passed before the empty cradle returned, allowing McKenzie and his remaining man to descend. Three of the officials returned to their limousine and drove away. The remaining two retired from the heat of day to the site office with another of McKenzie's team.

* * *

The cradle had been drawn up a short way to allow for more working space. At one side of it was suspended an electric lamp to compensate for a lack of daylight reaching the base of the shaft from the small square of blue sky high above. Should the winch operating the cradle jam, their only means of getting out was a series of metal ladders bolted at stages to the wall of the shaft. They could not call for assistance. There was no mobile phone signal. Close by the ladders ran an electric cable. This fed the hand-held console that assistant Steve Manning, its operator, had also plugged into the laptop computer placed nearby on the makeshift brick bench. 'Christ,' he mumbled, bending to switch on both console and computer, 'this isn't the easiest place to work.'

'Think yourself lucky,' responded McKenzie, 'those bloody officials didn't insist on coming down here with us. Who needs 'em!'

'Wouldn't be enough room with all this gear,' remarked second assistant, Craig Arnold, checking his camera.

During that morning, with a half hour break on the surface, they removed the clay seal with minimal damage than meticulously chipped the plaster away to free the door. A blaze of light accompanied each stage of the operation as Craig recorded it. They stared at the door a while then, with reverential care, McKenzie eased it back on its pivots to a grating sound and whisper of air. Set into timber frame and lintel, the door consisted of plain vertical boards held together by horizontal battens.

Beyond the door lay a gallery of utter, intimidating blackness.

The light of their torches revealed a stone passage hardly two metres in height, pierced at half its length on both sides by a doorway. Either side of each doorway were relief carvings, which, because of the narrow angle of view, could not be resolved. The passage, entirely free of debris, appeared to make an abrupt left turn at its far end.

'Looks as if this bloke knew what he was doing,' declared McKenzie. 'And deep down as it is, he must have considered one day someone would find the entrance. It reminds me of those movies where they find a lost tomb full of mantraps. Bloody weird.'

'That's it,' grinned Steve, 'pits full of sharpened stakes, boulders that roll out to crush you and spikes poking down from the ceiling.' His levity failed to disguise an underlying nervousness.

'Let's hope none of 'em are still working,' quipped Craig, though he shared the other's unease.

McKenzie reflected their feelings as he stared down the passage. 'It gives me the creeps,' he announced. 'All of a sudden I feel I'm in the wrong business.'

'I know what you mean,' admitted Craig. 'Now that door's open something tells me we should never have come down here. I was too damned hot before – now I'm getting the shivers. Must be the cold air spilling out of that gallery.'

Their voices, once confined by the walls of the shaft, reverberated within the gallery.

'Don't fret, mate,' assured Steve, 'young Snoopy here will be doing the dirty work.'

The robot, a small, tracked, black beetle-like machine, was equipped with laser rangefinder, lights and swivel-mounted stereo camera. It also carried ground sensors. It was attached to his console by a thin wire that would reel out as it went along.

'She's ready,' announced Steve glancing up from the console. 'Stand away from the door so we can let her through.' The machine hummed with life. LEDs glowed. Its diminutive headlamps shone brightly. The camera lenses rotated back and forth then its operator announced, 'Right, we are cleared for take-off.' As the robot whirred across the

14

threshold and entered the gallery he added, 'Ah - her rangefinder gives us nine metres twenty before the passage turns.'

'OK, Steve,' said McKenzie, gazing over his shoulder at the computer screen and seeing what the robot saw, 'have her nose about those two rooms first then we'll see what's around the corner.' As the robot continued on into the gallery he added, 'Great – we could be the first humans to get near the place in nearly five thousand years and here's a bloody machine doing the sightseeing.'

'Rather her than me,' muttered Craig as the robot turned into the left hand room. 'What're we seeing?' he asked, peering between the other two.

'Looks like an ante-room,' replied Steve. 'Not very big. Ah – there's a statue in the far corner. It's a human form in mummy wrappings and a skull cap?'

'The god, Ptah,' confirmed McKenzie. 'A popular bloke in those days.'

'What else are we seeing?' asked Craig.

'Jars,' replied McKenzie, 'decorated wooden chests, more jars, ornaments, still more bloody jars and what looks like a lot of furniture – most of it dismantled. It looks intact, though. Can't see any dust, sand or footprints. Even if there's nothing else down here, a find of this age is quite something.'

'Fantastic,' breathed Craig, feeling they and the robot had intruded into a forbidden place.

The plain-walled room and its contents drifted across the computer screen and the operator said, 'We've recorded a three-sixty degree sweep. Shall I take her across to the other room?'

'Better had, mate,' answered McKenzie. 'It's only a preliminary survey and we don't have too much time. Fergani will want it beamed direct to his office once we've some idea what we're in for. I 'ope he appreciates lots of jars.'

'He'll insist on being the first official down here as soon as he knows it's safe,' remarked Craig. 'Kudos and all that.'

The right-hand room was smaller but also proved to have plain walls, against which had been carefully placed more jars and chests. It was what lay at the far end of the room that caused McKenzie to gasp aloud, 'Stop her right there! Look at that!'

'More jars?' queried the second assistant.

'No, Craig, mummies – three of 'em,' replied McKenzie.'

The screen showed a trio of figures, each wrapped in part-decayed, grey bandages, each resting upright against the wall in an open casket of plain timber. Three more empty caskets stood nearby.

'No fancy coffins – just propped up there,' observed Craig. 'Sacrificial victims d'you think?'

McKenzie replied, 'Wouldn't like to guess, mate. As far as we know, human sacrifice in royal burials ended in the previous dynasty. But this – well -. Look, we'd better keep going so we can get out of here sooner rather than later.'

'I'll opt for sooner,' muttered Steve.

Emerging from the second room, the robot continued along to the end of the passage. On the screen its lights illuminated a blank wall where the gallery turned. The robot changed direction, disappeared around the corner then stopped.

'Sealed wooden doors straight ahead of her,' said McKenzie. 'Carved and decorated with hieroglyphs. That must lead to the main burial chamber but we're not going to find out what's in there until one of us goes through to open them.'

'You can volunteer, Don,' said Craig with an off-the-shelf smile.

'Shall I send her any further?' asked Steve, his hand poised over the joystick. 'Those doors are four metres ahead but I don't see anything in the way.'

McKenzie glanced at his watch. 'We ought to leave off now. The people upstairs will be busting a gut to see what we've found and this'll generate more bloody meetings. Bring our Snoopy back and we'll call it a day. We can leave most of the gear where it is.'

The robot reappeared, its lamps shining directly at them as a pair of malignant glowing eyes. They called down the cradle and were soon ascending toward welcome daylight.

***

Camera at the ready, Stacey watched them approach the gateway in the fence where stood the two armed guards. 'Hey, you guys!' he called as they passed through. 'What gives? What did you find in there?'

McKenzie, laptop in hand, paused to reply, 'Sorry, mate, but there's nothing to wet your pants over. Nothing we can tell anyone at this time.'

The two officials from the site office were already waiting close by but Stacey persisted. 'Is it the tomb of Imhotep? Is it intact? Just give me a "yes" or a "no," can't you?'

McKenzie ignored him, muttering, 'How the hell did he guess that?'

Stacey turned back to the fence. A portable cabin had been set up behind it a few metres from the shaft. For a long time he stared at this, convinced there was a scoop to be had here. A big scoop.

***

From behind his polished mahogany desk the portly, bearded Dr Fergani, Director of Antiquities, reviewed the scene recorded by the robot. 'How certain can we be that this is the tomb of Imhotep?'

'We've good reason to believe it is,' replied McKenzie, 'at least at this point. But until the inner doors are opened we can't be one hundred percent. And it's always possible thieves entered the tomb in ancient times by another route. We can't discount that even if the ante-rooms are untouched.'

Dr Fergani turned from the now blank screen. 'I wish to see this for myself – before other people go down there. It could be of great national importance but as you are aware these are troubled times. We must be careful.'

'The quieter we keep this the better,' agreed McKenzie, recalling outbreaks of sectarian violence in Cairo. 'That arsehole of a reporter is hanging around. He's convinced he's onto something because of the activity around the shaft. He's already guessed it could be Imhotep – how I can't say. A few misplaced words from any of us could have the whole world rolling in.'

'Ah, yes, Mr Stacey. He has caused our department some embarrassment in the past. I have been endeavouring to have his permit revoked but these things take time and he has so far not broken any laws. Shall we plan my arrival for ten o'clock tomorrow morning?'

'Ten in the morning it is,' replied McKenzie.

***

The Director stepped from his limousine trailed by two plain-clothed police – their status hinted at by rugged build, immaculately tailored suits and designer sunglasses. McKenzie and his first assistant helped Fergani into the cradle but the Director of Antiquities, confronted by the gaping depths of the shaft, appeared to relinquish much of his enthusiasm. Stacey, anonymous amidst a small group of tourists gathered some way beyond the fence, watched three hardhats drop from view.

More lights had been lowered into the shaft so that the restricted area at its base, the robot and other paraphernalia were better illuminated. McKenzie and his assistant explained the basic functions of the robot, reminding the Director of how such machines had earlier been employed to good effect inside the Great Pyramid of Khufu at Giza.

The Director, his smart-suited presence totally anomalous stared uneasily into the horizontal gallery whose far end was obscured in darkness, then at the diminutive patch of sky above, partly obscured by the cradle. 'Do we know if the passage is safe?' he asked.

'As far along as the robot's been we believe it is,' answered McKenzie, noting the man's discomfort. 'Are we authorised to proceed further now you've seen it for yourself?'

Taking a deep breath the Director again glanced upward then replied, 'I wish to return to the site office. Let us discuss matters there.' Dr Fergani was sweating visibly.

'Are you feeling OK, sir?' asked Steve.

'I do not like enclosed spaces,' answered the Director. 'I did not realise how oppressive it would be down here.'

It took some minutes for the cradle to reach the surface, during which time the Director gripped hard on the safety rail and remained silent. Stacey, watching through binoculars, observed his expression of anxiety as the hardhat was lifted from him.

Joined by Craig and the two escorts, all six were on their way to the site office when Craig said, 'While you were down there I saw our pal Stacey hanging about with his camera and spyglasses. He's up to something.'

'Well he would be, wouldn't he,' responded McKenzie, eyeing the Director. 'I hope your men will see the nosey bugger doesn't get any closer.'

'They have their orders,' responded the Director. 'If Stacey or anyone else attempts to enter the site they will be arrested at once and taken to Cairo.'

Inside the site office Dr Fergani seemed more relaxed and after further discussion on the subject of the excavation, said, 'I suggest that we send no one in there until your machine has undertaken a more detailed survey of those two rooms and their contents. I think also that it should look closer at that sealed door. Do you agree?'

'Sure,' answered McKenzie. 'I'd like to start first thing tomorrow so we can examine the ante-rooms in more detail and produce an accurate plan. The rest of today I could use in keying in notes on what we've done so far.'

'Yes - yes, I think so,' agreed the Director.

***

There was only one guard visible inside the compound that moonless night where there should have been two. He stood leaning against the gatepost, pistol at his waist, the stub of a cigarette teetering on his lower lip. A petrol generator ran noisily to power five halogen floodlights spaced about the fence. Voices and laughter could be heard from within the temporary cabin. As Stacey approached the site the guard threw aside his cigarette.

'Hi there,' announced Stacey, stepping up to the gate. 'You speak English?'

'I speak some,' replied the guard, eyeing him suspiciously through the wire netting.

'Take one of my cigarettes,' offered Stacey, withdrawing his own packet and holding it close to the netting. The guard pushed fingers through to accept the cigarette. Stacey watched him light it then said, 'Take them all. I've got plenty.' The guard appeared reluctant until Stacey insisted with a smile, 'Go on, pal – they're yours.' Stacey watched him pocket the cigarettes then asked, 'You like your job? Does it pay well?'

'I have my family to feed. I must do this job.'

'Look, pal, what's the big deal here? Why all the security and the fence?'

The guard exhaled a stream of smoke then replied, 'I do not know what they have found but we are told not to speak to people.'

'Then it must be important – good as Tutankhamun, maybe? But you have to keep your word, I understand that - so don't talk about anything. Just let me inside – OK?'

'No I cannot do that. I have sworn on the holy Koran.'

Stacey reached into his safari coat pocket and produced a number of large denomination bank notes. 'See this? Open this gate for a second or two and look the other way and it's all yours. I don't want anyone else involved – get my meaning? No one else at all. If I see what I want to see then there'll be more cash in it for you, I promise. But you never saw me here. If anything happens, I must have crawled through underneath the fence – right?'

The guard wide-eyed the banknotes as Stacey splayed them out. He bit his lip, then looking furtively about, reached for his keys and unlocked the gate. Stacey pushed through and handed over the cash, saying, 'You won't regret this, pal.' When the guard had relocked the gate Stacey asked, 'OK, how do I get down there?'

'There is a thing that goes up and down,' hissed the guard, glancing anxiously beyond the fence. 'It makes a noise so you cannot use that. There is a ladder but down there is very deep.'

'How deep?'

Shadows moved across the lighted window of the site cabin. Voices sounded louder. The guard, clearly agitated, replied, 'Please, mister, you should not be here!'

'OK, I'll get going.' Stacey trudged over to the shaft and, clutching the side of the cradle, peered down into blackness. From one pocket he withdrew his camera. This he switched on, confirming for a third time since setting out that night that the battery was charged. Dropping the camera back into his pocket he pulled from the other an electric torch and shone its beam down into the shaft. 'Jesus Christ,' he muttered, 'Where the hell's the bottom?'

His torch picked out the ladder where it hung to the left side of the cradle. Stacey moved around then peered once again into the shaft. His confidence was shaken by the prospect of entering but he would not retreat from what might prove the chance of a lifetime. He looked around to see the guard watching from by the gate. Returning the torch to his pocket he gripped the cradle rail and lowered his left foot tentatively over the edge until his toe engaged a rung of the ladder. 'This has got to be worth it,' he muttered, swinging down his right leg to locate the next rung. He paused with both hands grasping the sides of the ladder. For over a minute he stared across to the gate. The guard had not moved.

The stars above shone with rare intensity and Mike Stacey began his long descent into blackness.

**

Two men entered the cradle shortly after nine o'clock the next morning. On reaching the bottom, McKenzie stood aside whilst Steve, having activated the robot, had it whirring softly over the threshold on its second journey into the gallery.

'Don,' he said, gazing after the robot as it approached the left hand doorway, 'each time we come down here I like it less than the time before. I've been in some pretty odd spots – but this -.'

'I know what you mean, mate, it's affected all of us - but try not to let it get at you the way it did Fergani. I'll bet he won't be coming down again.'

'Let's hope not,' agreed his assistant. 'Ah – we're at the entrance to the first room.'

'Right, let's have the little treasure explore every nook and cranny and get some detailed images. Let her take her time before we go into that second room. I've a feeling this could be our last opportunity the way things are going in Cairo.'

'I'll programme her to run on autopilot. That'll make life easier and give us a couple of hours and more upstairs until the next room - unless you prefer to stay with it.'

'No thanks,' responded McKenzie, 'Do what you have to do and let's get out of here.'

At the surface both men joined Craig at the site office. There they speculated upon the possible discoveries that might lie ahead if or when it was decided they should enter that last portal.

After two hours McKenzie and his small team returned to the site where he glanced about and remarked, 'Have you noticed anything? Looks as if our Mr Stacey's fallen out with us. I don't recall seeing the bugger when we first arrived, either.'

'We all know how much you miss him,' grinned Craig.

'Oh, I do,' glowered McKenzie. 'Like a boil on the arse! Perhaps he went back into Cairo and got himself mixed up in the disturbances. We can but hope!'

Steve glanced at his watch. 'Let's get down there and see if she's ready to do that next room.'

***

It was close on three-thirty when the robot completed its survey of the second room. McKenzie and his assistant had returned some ten minutes before and McKenzie decided they should next explore the full length of the hidden passage. The robot had disappeared from view when a signal sounded from the console.

'What's up?' asked McKenzie.

'Her sensors indicate a problem with the floor. I'll have her track from side to side and see if we can get around it.'

'What d'you mean, a problem?'

Steve gazed intently at the console then answered, 'The floor's no longer solid and she's still over a metre from the door.' A minute passed before he added, 'It's possibly a hidden shaft. She isn't finding any way around it. Could be some kind of trap. If it is then the floor may not hold her weight.'

'Damn,' breathed McKenzie. 'Better bring her back. We daren't take any risks.'

With the robot on its return journey, Steve said, 'She can stay down here until we know our next move. I'll just bring the laptop.'

'You got any recordable disks for that?' asked McKenzie.

'Yes, I've a couple in the case – why?'

'Dig 'em out. I want to back up and keep everything we've recorded in here – right now.'

'But why? We'll be going through it all with Fergani and it's strictly confidential.'

'Maybe so,' responded McKenzie, 'but if things do get worse in Cairo, Fergani will close the operation and confiscate everything. We'll keep a separate record of our own since it's our university funding this operation.'

'OK, but close that door first - my flesh just started crawling!'

***

In the Director of Antiquities' committee room Dr Fergani and three officials sat before the big screen to witness for the first time moving images from the second survey. Also present were McKenzie and his two assistants. Now and again Fergani would ask for a scene to be freeze-framed and comments or questions would issue from one or more of his staff. At one point, in the final sequence from the second ante-room, McKenzie jerked upright in his chair, hand raised as if about to speak.

'You wish to explain something?' asked the Director.

'Er, no – no, I don't,' McKenzie replied after some hesitation. 'Just – yes, just carry on.'

McKenzie remained preoccupied, saying nothing more until the playback had ended.

Outside the committee room Dr Fergani turned to him. 'You have been away from the news whilst working at Saqqara. We have had increasing violence here in Cairo.'

'We know all about that,' responded McKenzie. 'We're not stuck underground all the time.'

'Of course not - but because of this I now must order all further work on the tomb halted.' Fergani waited for a response. McKenzie said nothing so the

Director continued, 'Should law and order break down such an important site will be a target for looters. The shaft is to be refilled and members of our armed forces will be stationed nearby. Nobody concerned with these operations is to speak of what has been so far discovered and nothing must be published. Is that understood?'

'I hear what you say,' replied McKenzie. 'Oh, I left some of my papers on the table. I'll go back for 'em then we'll be off.'

**

His assistants returned to the site office to find an uncharacteristically grave Don McKenzie seated at his desk.

'What happened back there?' asked Steve as they drew up their chairs. 'Some of us noticed the expression on your face during the show but you kept quiet.'

'Yes - I did, didn't I,' replied McKenzie. 'I've downloaded two stills from that disk – one from the preliminary survey and one from the second. Both of 'em from the right-hand ante-room. There's something I want you blokes to see that no one in the meeting noticed.'

McKenzie swung the monitor around. Both men studied the screen as he switched the images back and forth. 'OK,' said Craig at last, 'what's happened here?'

'Yes, Don,' added the other man. 'Who's been buggering about with these images?'

'No one's been buggering about with anything, mate. No one's laid a finger on 'em!'

'But,' said Steve, 'the image from the second survey shows another -.'

'Yes, Steve, and yes, Craig, there are only three mummies in the first image but four in the second! You both see that, don't you? There's a fourth mummy in one of those empty caskets!' McKenzie zoomed in on the image. 'And tell me what you think that is laying close to that fourth mummy – there, see, just visible on the floor.'

'Jesus Christ,' breathed Craig, 'it's a camera.'

'It looks like the camera I saw Stacey's carrying,' said the other.

'It *is* Stacey's camera!' snapped McKenzie. 'I've seen him waving the thing at us often enough. The silly bugger went down there last night and I've a feeling he won't be coming back. In fact I know he won't!'

'Stacey himself must have rigged this,' shrugged Steve. 'If not then I don't understand.'

'Nor me,' added Craig.

'And I don't want to even try!' exclaimed Don McKenzie, slamming his hand on the desk. 'We're supposed to be rational, professional men,' he continued, 'but down there we got involved with something we ought not to be involved with, and if word of it ever gets out we'll each end up looking for another job. Wouldn't our Mr Stacey have loved this one if some other idiot had sneaked in there instead of him.'

'But won't someone at the Department notice next time that disk is played?' asked Steve.

'No they won't,' replied McKenzie, relaxing in his chair. 'I slipped back into their committee room after the meeting and grabbed it. Apart from my disk and your laptop there's no other copy. If they ask, we scrubbed our hard drive clean to ensure security. It's what Fergani wanted and I doubt he'll care to make a fuss over the missing disk.'

'Can't get my head around this one,' said Craig. 'Either we've been conned or you've helped preserve the secrets of a five thousand year old man.'

'Maybe so – but the sooner they refill that damned shaft and cover the site over the better. Oh, and Steve – you'll need to go down there again to bring out the robot. She *is* your responsibility!'

Whispers

The silver hatchback pulled into a lay-by, its tyre tracks exposing dark asphalt from under a thin covering of snow. The engine murmured smoothly, the gentle breath of the air conditioning system provided comforting warmth that enabled the frigid scene beyond the car windows to appear somewhat picturesque. To the right, exposed hills swept up into misted greyness. To the left, beyond the lay-by, the level land was thickly populated with bare winter trees. He gazed a while into the snow-brushed woods and saw only more trees beyond. He was becoming impatient. The day ought to have been routine but it was turning out otherwise.

Pulling his iPhone from the glove compartment he called up the map showing his location, noted the weak signal warning then keyed in a number. 'Hi, it's Darren Connor. Is that James?'

The voice was none too clear but it was James.

'James you're breaking up – can you hear me OK?' … 'Great. I'm out in the sticks on the Chapelbury road but I can't find this bloody house. There's no turn-off shown on the map and I can't find one between the main road and Chapelbury itself.' … 'No, there isn't even a pub – just a few houses and an old church. I've been up there and back three times and it's hardly a village at all. There's not a pub or a garage for miles around.' … 'OK, I'll hang on.'

He continued to stare along the deserted road then the voice returned. He listened for a half minute then replied, 'That means I have to look for a bloody farm track does it? Just as well I brought a coat. It's arctic out here, I can tell you – maybe OK on a Christmas card if you like that kind of thing. How the hell can the office not find out if anyone lives there? It isn't the Middle Ages for Christ's sake. Someone must hold deeds to the land. The local council or the land registry should have turned up something'… 'Well maybe they didn't try hard enough' … 'Sure, you get out and enjoy yourself - and have one on me you lucky bugger!'

The radio volume had been lowered before he made the call but now he turned it up. Cool jazz was playing. Not the kind of cool that surrounded him beyond the plush comfort of the company vehicle he presently enjoyed. Darren had no wish to leave the car.

The zippered folder resting on the passenger seat bore his company logo in gold and blue against fine-grained black leather. He opened and withdrew from it a set of papers including one showing plans of the area. This he laid aside before leaning back to study the details that summed up the reason for his journey. It confirmed the woods were privately owned and that residents might possibly live close by. It revealed no more than that so he returned to the sheet bearing the map. It indicated clearly enough the road he was on as well as the hamlet several kilometres back. He checked his navigator screen to confirm his position as being roughly half way between Chapelbury and the main road laying in the opposite direction.

'Hm,' he muttered, peering at the printed map, 'it has to be nearby. Looks like it's through the woods from roughly about here – and that could be a path further along.'

He switched off the engine, contemplated the uneasy silence for some moments then opened the car door to an unwelcome shock of raw, chilling air. Less welcome still as he strode around to the rear, lifted the hatch, dragged out and pulled on his coat then collected up his laptop computer. Having closed the hatch, having locked the car with the remote control key, he glanced about, certain he had not passed a proper turn-off since leaving the main road. He looked down at his shoes, concerned that he might have to walk across rough ground although the snow appeared smooth and clean.

A dilapidated dry-stone wall followed that stretch of the road he was on and some way along he observed a gap with what could be a path of sorts just beyond. He trudged the few steps to the gap before looking over his shoulder at the car and the deserted road. An absence of tyre tracks told him this was not a well-frequented route.

At either side of the gap stood a tilted, lichen-encrusted square stone pillar, the right hand one of the pair showing evidence that it had long ago supported a gate. The route beyond was thickly wooded, the trees mature, their leafless winter branches stark against a bleak sky and spreading out far enough, even though bare, to create a brooding, twilight vault. He proceeded through, treading along a vague track defined only by the wider spacing of trees and undergrowth, noting there was no evidence of footprints to indicate anyone had recently passed that way. He noted also that, because he had wasted time earlier, the winter sun was lower in the sky than he wished it had been and the mist had descended to spread through the trees as a layer of chilling haze.

'God,' he muttered, pulling his coat tighter and turning up the collar, 'how the hell can anyone not be known to the authorities even in this part of the world? I hope whatever I'm looking for turns out to be empty so I can be away from here soon.'

Although the route he was taking through the woods was ill defined, only a minute or so passed before the trees began to spread out. The woods soon gave way to more open land where grassy hummocks protruded through frozen whiteness. Then he saw the house - a grey smudge against a darker backdrop of crowding trees. He might have assumed it to be deserted were not thin wisps of smoke rising lazily from the chimney into still air. 'Oh, damn,' he breathed, eyeing his watch, 'there *is* someone living there.'

Treading uneven ground he approached a small, two-storey farm building with glistening wet slate roof and small, mullioned windows set into thick stone walls. The house, he concluded, must be very old. A short way to the right of the house were stone outbuildings; stables at one time, perhaps, but these appeared dilapidated and overgrown. The decaying ruins of a black wooden barn with doors hanging askew could be seen further back. The windows of the house looked blank as he stepped up to a front door of plain, gnarled wooden planks studded at intervals with rusted iron bolt-heads. The ring-shaped iron knocker was cold and stiff as he tapped it against the door. The reverberating hollow thud might have come from an empty cavern.

There was no response. His breath rose in pale wisps and he was feeling chilled through and through in spite of a heavy coat.

'With a bit of luck they'll be out or stone deaf,' he muttered, glancing aside at the bleak landscape. 'Next time around someone else can make the effort.'

He stepped back intending to peer into the nearest window when the front door clicked and sighed half way open. A woman's face appeared from the dim interior. She was elderly, slightly built and possessing thick, straight white hair swept back to a bun.

'Ah, sorry to bother you,' he began, 'I'm Darren Connor from Fairmont Properties. Er, I need to speak with the owner or owners of this property if that's at all possible.' She continued to stare at him as he added, 'We wanted to contact them but we've been unable to locate an address or phone number even through the local council.'

He was already feeling like an intruder when the door opened further and a man's face appeared behind hers; rounded, weather-beaten and with thinning white hair.

'Young man from a property company,' said the woman in an oddly accented voice, turning to the one who had just joined her. 'Says 'e wants to talk to us.'

'Wants to talk to us, does he?' grated the old man. 'Better have 'im in then.'

The door opened wider and the two moved back, allowing their visitor enough space to enter. He stepped by them with some difficulty, bending to avoid the low doorframe to find himself within a narrow dimly lit hallway. The two pushed by and the old man gestured for him to stoop through the first door on his right. Was this the house he'd been looking for? Even now he was not entirely certain. He noted their attire – plain and simple, as if their lives never took them into town or city. In his professional capacity he was accustomed to evaluating the possessions and likely income of others and wondered what there might be to appraise in his present surroundings.

At the opposite side of a small room with plain, white-plastered walls and timber-beamed ceiling, flames leapt brightly from logs set beneath the arch of a rough-hewn stone fireplace. The small windows to his right were hung with drab curtains that allowed only meagre light from the declining day beyond. A pair of muted green, plainly upholstered high-backed chairs and a two-seater of similar style were positioned close by the windows. In the centre of the room stood a small but stout, plain oak table and a pair of rustic chairs. On an ancient oak dresser to the left were arrayed earthenware plates and dishes of a type he would have expected to find on the shelves of an antique shop in some country village. Positioned lower down on small white dishes were two, plain wax candles, their flames wavering in disturbed air.

He noted the absence of a radio or television, even of electric lighting. There was no switch on the wall. There was no light fitting on the ceiling. A few pictures hung about the walls – the largest of them above the fireplace. Plain, coarse-woven matting covered an otherwise bare wooden floor.

The room ought to have been warm and cosy. He did not find it so.

'I'm awfully sorry to bother you,' he said, 'but I've had a real job of it trying to locate this property and it is rather important. Are there any other houses in the vicinity?'

'Better sit down, lad,' said the old man, gesturing to the nearest of the chairs that stood tucked beneath the table then adding, 'There's nowt else around 'ere.'

As he dragged back a chair, Darren wondered if they ever had visitors since they appeared ill-equipped to entertain anyone. He glanced down to see if the chair was clean, then sat, as did the old man. The woman remained standing. Neither had suggested he remove his coat and so it stayed on despite the presence of a fire; a fire that in any case seemed to give out little if any heat. They continued to stare at him. That made him feel uncomfortable, so he placed the zip folder and laptop on the table, saying, 'I'd much appreciate it if you could confirm that you are the owners of this property.'

'This 'ouse has been in our family for generations,' the old man informed him. 'The Northcotts, y'know. I'm Thomas and my wife 'ere is Alice. Our ancestors once farmed this land; now there's no need of it.'

'Well, Mr Northcott – Mrs Northcott, I'll get straight to the point: we had to find out if the land was still occupied because my company wishes to purchase these fields for development and -.'

'For development?' interrupted Mr Northcott. 'What d'you mean by that?'

'Well, what we have in mind is a leisure centre with accommodation, restaurant and health spa. It would be ideal for people wishing to tour the area and great, of course, for those keen on walking. There would have to be a link road and car parking facilities, naturally.'

'Naturally,' repeated Mr Northcott.

'Naturally,' murmured his wife.

On hearing the less than reassuring tone in their voices, Darren reached to open the laptop, saying, 'Look, allow me to show you what we have in mind.' He switched the computer on, adding with an off-the-shelf smile, 'It is not company policy to spoil anything unnecessarily. In any case we have to be pretty careful with our proposals nowadays. Don't want to upset the environmentalists.'

He was nevertheless confident his proposals would be of interest since the Northcott's standard of living and lack of even basic modern amenities indicated a wholly inadequate financial situation.

The glowing screen cast a swath of light across the table. He pressed a few keys and a plan of the area appeared together with a representation of the buildings and car park.

Mr Northcott stared at the screen without a change of expression. 'Is that road on the right the one you came 'ere by?' he asked.

'Yes, it's the road to Chapelbury.'

'So that – that place you're talking about - it looks to be where we are now.'

'That's correct, Mr Northcott,' confirmed their visitor. 'This is an open area so it would minimise the clearing of woodland. I doubt the local authority would be happy about that anyway.'

'So you'll want to knock us 'ouse down.'

Darren hesitated before replying. 'Er - that would be the case but I notice much of the property is already derelict and,' he peered briefly about the room as if to emphasise his message, 'and if I'm not mistaken you don't have any modern facilities; not even electricity.'

'We're plenty comfortable as we are,' said Mrs Northcott. 'We're a part of this 'ouse.'

'I do understand but if I may say so, you probably will in the future require a home with modern amenities and greater comforts – electric lights, central heating, a telephone, etcetera. In addition to the full purchase price of your house and land we can offer you an extremely good deal. A new home would be made available to you at company expense. It would be fully furnished and conveniently located for shops and medical services. We have a smallish but attractive new development already underway at Kelthorpe. Perfect for the senior citizen.'

'And you need us permission to use this land, I take it,' said Mr Northcott.

'Well if you *are* the legal owners – then yes, we do.'

'And if we don't care to give that permission?'

'If that were so – it would, er, it would then be out of my hands. Look,' he continued, unzipping the folder, 'I have the paperwork here detailing our proposals. Perhaps you'd care to take a look at it. I have no wish at all to apply pressure but it would be in your best interests to consider our offer very seriously. We will arrange a further visit to see if we can progress matters. You may wish to obtain legal advice.'

'Would we now,' breathed Mr Northcott.'

Without illumination from the laptop, wording on the paperwork would have been illegible. Throughout their conversation Mrs Northcott had remained standing and continued to stare at him whilst showing no interest in the computer screen. He found her steady gaze increasingly unnerving. Mr Northcott drew the papers across the table as if to study them. The atmosphere was tense, the fire blazed brighter as the old man gazed hard at documents he appeared not to be reading. Their visitor occupied himself in peering at the computer screen.

An eternity of minutes had passed when Mrs Northcott asked, 'Would you care for tea and buttered scones?'

'Oh, er, yes,' he replied, wanting to appear amiable then glancing at his watch and wishing he had answered, 'No.'

Mr Northcott got up and accompanied his wife to the kitchen, saying, 'We'll talk on it now if you'll wait a while.'

Left alone, he had no desire to remain within the house. He could not, of course, express his opinion that the Northcotts were people of little consequence in the modern world but he had already reached that conclusion. He looked around the room to see if there were any newspapers or magazines scattered about. There were none. Nor was there even a clock. He wondered how they obtained their shopping and those day-to-day necessities everyone nowadays took for granted.

It occurred to him how, with no electricity or gas, the shadows would close in when darkness fell; reaching throughout the house with probing tentacles of blackness spreading from every corner. The Northcott's isolated world would resemble a candle-lit mausoleum in a gulf of boundless night. He was reassured by the presence of those items of modern technology carried with him into this strange, out of time house. Had it not been for the laptop standing here on the table and the feel of the phone in his pocket, he might have doubted this was the twenty-first century. Time seemed of no importance to these people – but it was so to him. Once again he glanced at his watch, once again at the window.

The light beyond was waning.

His attention returned to the pictures – in particular to the one above the fireplace. He got up and stepped across the room, noting with a sideways glimpse the small farmhouse kitchen with wood burning stove and several more lighted candles. The Northcotts stood with their backs to him. The fire, blazing brightly as before, struck him as odder still because it never seemed to change.

In the dim light the picture showed a young, attractive girl wearing bonnet and rustic dress of an earlier century. She was seated by a tree from which a setting sun cast long shadows. In the background stood the house in which he now was, with thick smoke coiling from the chimney. There were the outbuildings, all intact, but there was no wooden barn. He assumed the picture must have been painted before the barn was constructed. The girl looked oddly familiar, not unlike Mrs Northcott despite the difference in age, so he concluded this must be an ancestor of hers. On the girl's knee rested an open book, its pages tilted toward the viewer. The wording on the nearest page was just legible so he strained to read what was evidently a verse.

The evening beacon of the sun
Glorious in its demise
Bestirs the spirits of the earth
That stalk the wilderness of night.

They were words he would at any other time have skimmed over and dismissed. Now he found them disturbing. 'This place is getting to me,' he muttered, once more reaching to touch the phone in his pocket. About to return to the chair he was startled to find the Northcotts staring at him from close by the table. A cup and plate rested close by his laptop and zip folder so when Mr Northcott sat down Darren reluctantly re-joined them. Mrs Northcott occupied her former position, standing by the table.

The laptop now seemed a gross intruder so he switched off, closed and placed it together with his folder down by the side of his chair. Candle and firelight would have to suffice. The fire danced, hissed and whispered. An odd sound; it reminded him of many hushed voices in furtive conversation. It threw their shadows up large across the wall at the end of the room where the door to the hallway stood. He imagined the house must be full of alcoves, of secret spaces, and that upstairs must be forbidding, cold and dark.

To consume the modest offering whilst they watched was much to his discomfort and it occurred to him he was somehow being manipulated. He, the company man, was used to being in charge of a situation. Here, in this charged silence, he felt he no longer was, though he still hoped to elicit a spark of interest over his proposals. Having finished the tea but only one of the scones he asked, 'How d'you manage – I mean for groceries or, or anything like that?'

'We 'ave no problems,' replied Mrs Northcott.

'None at all,' added her husband.

'But you're so isolated here and without transport. You must need to access local services from time to time. Do any buses run this way?'

Mr Northcott smiled weakly. It was the first time either of them had smiled as the old man replied, 'We manage. Always 'ave.'

'That's so,' agreed Mrs Northcott. 'We manage. Yes, we always 'ave.'

Further silence ensued. A silence broken only by the whispering fire.

'OK,' said their visitor, glancing again at his watch, 'I ought to be leaving now.' Turning to look at the window he wished he had uttered those words earlier. The sky outside had deepened beyond twilight. 'I strongly recommend you consider our proposals,' he added with a smile he hoped would disguise his impatience. 'It really is quite generous. I'll leave the paperwork with you to read over properly and then phone up to – oh, you don't have a telephone here, do you?'

'Nothing like that,' answered Mr Northcott.

'Then can I arrange another -?'

We're always 'ere,' interrupted Mrs Northcott. 'Always.'

'Yes,' added Mr Northcott, 'always 'ere – should you come by again.'

The company man reached for his computer and folder then arose from the chair. Mr Northcott stood also and both followed him to the hallway. Darren opened the front door and stepped out into the night, his breath clouding before his face as he turned to say goodbye, though he had no wish to shake their hands. Two faces regarded him from around the part closed door. Both now were smiling as Mrs Northcott said, 'Perhaps we'll be seeing you again, dear. As Thomas and I mentioned - we're always at home.'

The door closed to a hollow thud.

The sky was clear but almost dark. A half-moon vaguely illuminated the snow through mists that had thickened noticeably since his arrival. Darren stared across the field but the trees through which he'd earlier passed were no longer visible and his footprints were unclear on pitted ground close to the house. 'God,' he muttered, 'I should have got out of there sooner. Weird bloody pair – relics from another age.'

He recalled the direction from which he had earlier approached the house and set off accordingly, his shoes crunching snow. 'And that house – how the hell could anyone live there? Now - that gap in the woods – it has to be that way.'

He peered ahead, continued on in the cold until the woods loomed, but on drawing closer the phalanx of trees and undergrowth of bushes before him stood dark and impenetrable. Clutching the laptop and folder he stopped to look about. Of the pathway through the trees there was no sign.

'Damn,' he breathed, peering into the mist, 'I must have gone in the wrong direction.'

He turned to his left and walked on, all the time straining to discover a way through but finding none. 'This is bloody ridiculous! The path's got to be around here somewhere.'

There was no breeze but he became aware of a sound. A whispering like that of the fire in the house. He imagined something hovered beyond his vision in the mist and for the first time since childhood he experienced a fear of darkness..

'What *are* those sounds?' he murmured. 'There must be an animal around here. A horse or a dog, something panting - maybe a fox – yes, that's what it'll be.' Again he stopped and his breath drifted on freezing air. 'Never mind that - I've got to find the damned car. Can't be far away.'

The mist had begun to obscure even the closer trees and he was becoming disorientated. He turned about and, able on smoother ground to make out his new footprints, strode back the way he had come, all the time aware of the sounds.

'I must have walked too far over – that's it. The path has to be further along this way.'

Peering down, he came at last to footprints showing where he had turned left so he continued on past these only to find some twenty steps ahead more trees emerging from the mist. He stopped, looked around then retraced his steps, acutely anxious now over the whispering that seemed to follow him. Was it drawing closer?

'Is anybody there?' he called, staring into frigid obscurity.

Delving into his coat pocket he pulled out the remote locking device. This he pointed toward the trees, repeatedly pressing the unlock button in the hope that he might be close enough to make the lights of his car flash on and off in the mist and show him which way to go. There was no response. 'Where's my damned car!' he cried aloud, though the mist deadened his voice. 'Is anybody out there? Can anyone hear me?'

There was only the whispering.

Darren hurried away from the trees – away from the direction he thought he had been taking. On he trudged, surrounded by impenetrable night. 'Christ, there's got to be an end to this! Where's that damned house? Where?' Gripping laptop and folder under one arm he stopped to pull out his phone. 'I'll key in my co-ordinates – that's it, yes. I'll call for help before I freeze to death –the police, maybe.'

He peered in despair at the phone. The read-out indicated, "No Signal."

The whispering grew more persistent, swirling from the mists all about, seeming to emerge from one direction then another, advancing then receding. Eyes darting from side to side, breath shortening, he stumbled on, clutching ever harder to those tokens of reason and sanity that had so far held in check the full spate of elemental fear. Yet panic now threatened to become his master.

A vague form loomed ahead of him. 'Ah, it's that bloody house!' he gasped. 'They can get up off their arses and help me. I don't care if they've gone to bed, either. That old bugger can come down right now and show me the way out of this mess!'

He strode closer. There was no light showing. Smoke no longer arose from the chimney.

Grasping the iron ring he knocked hard on the door, then after a few seconds harder still.

'Come on, come on,' he muttered. But there was the whispering, seeming now only a few steps away. Moving aside to the window he pressed his face against cold, cracked glass but could see nothing. 'Open up will you!' he called glancing over his shoulder. 'Answer the door!'

He stepped back to the door, the laptop and folder almost slipping from his grasp. The whispering followed. His flesh crawled as he hammered hard against solid timber. He was startled when the door swung inward to reveal not a human figure but only darkness. With a backward glance he pushed into the hallway and slammed the door shut. The whispering stopped and there was silence. Utter silence. On the air hung an odour of damp decay he had not been aware of when first invited into the house. He stood listening for a time, hoping someone would appear, then called aloud toward stairs he had earlier noticed further along the passage, 'Hello! Are you there! Can you hear me!'

His voice reverberated into obscurity. Numb with cold, chilled by fear, he remained by the door for a measure of heartbeats then repeated his call – this time louder. Still there was no reply.

There was a vague glow on the wall ahead, opposite the room where he had spent time in conversation with the Northcotts. The fire must still be burning. He trod cautiously to where the door stood ajar. Perhaps they were resting in their chairs. Perhaps they needed to take medication to make them sleep and were oblivious to his calling. He would be cautious. Pushing the door further in he called softly, 'Hello,' then entered.

By the light of the fire he could see there was no one in the room. He could see also that it was altogether empty. The walls were flaking and cracked, the pictures and furniture gone, the floor bare except for scattered fragments of plaster and swathes of grit. 'What!' he cried aloud, clutching computer and folder to his chest. 'What's happened here? Where the hell are you?'

He stepped open-mouthed to the fire that gave no heat. The room was bitterly cold, yet the fire blazed with increasing ferocity. It illuminated his features as a gaping mask. It cast his shadow to sway across crumbling wall and sagging ceiling. The fire whispered as it had before, as the whispering in the mist but here with reptile hiss. It gushed as if it might leap from beneath the chimney. He stared mesmerised into the fire, seeing it form whorls and spirals that grew to become intricate, impossible convolutions. In those patterns two faces appeared, their features defined by coiling flames. The Northcotts peered up at him in burning mockery, their features quivering smiles. He cried out, dropped the laptop and folder then fled horror-stricken from the room into the darkness of the hallway. There he staggered blindly, wrenched open the front door and stumbled out into the mist. On he blundered, arms outstretched, whilst the whispering coiled about to become insane laughter. On he went into impenetrable mist. On into nameless night.

***

'Hi, Darren, it's James here again. Tried to get you earlier, mate. We're closing the office now so I'll say again - in case you haven't already quit looking, don't bother. We finally tracked down the info. No one occupies that land. The property was abandoned generations ago and the land left in the hands of some defunct private trust. Call me at home later if you want the full details. Otherwise, hope you had a good day and have a pleasant evening!'

Allure

It was a week of frustration. A week of scant progress on his current novel when ideas for the final chapter should have been in full bloom. The plot of the book was mainly laid out, all the players in the drama established in their roles, particularly that of the young woman with green eyes, but the very ending refused to gel. He would for a time dismiss from his mind the all too persistent characters and, reinforced by a large Scotch, stare at something other than computer screen text. Late that drizzling afternoon he climbed into his car with no greater aim in mind than to browse the town shopping centre.

It was his first visit to the centre, though it seemed oddly familiar. He strolled aimlessly past open doors, turning here and there through shop-lined arcades, in and out of numerous stores until becoming quite disorientated. Bright and bustling when he first arrived, the shopping centre was now emptying. The few people still about were a tide receding from him in every direction. He entered a shop to pause amidst settings of household furniture arranged as though the occupants had left only moments before. He stood motionless for a time and in that time the surroundings pressed upon him as a surreal theatre, an abandoned stage set. He stepped into an adjacent, smaller room where easy chairs and a settee were set invitingly about before a fireplace where flames danced. Real flames or so they appeared. On the mantelpiece stood china ornaments and a glass-domed clock with busy little pendulum flickering light. About the walls hung framed, monochrome pictures depicting young women of pre-war appearance. There were no shop assistants in sight. There had been music playing earlier. Now there was a charged silence he felt he ought not to disturb.

Glancing at his watch he knew it had to be closing time, though he'd heard no announcement. He left the shop and walked on, looking for exit signs, finding none, seeing no one to stop and ask, eventually fancying himself alone in some rambling maze; a deserted labyrinth with no means of escape until it opened again the following day. He'd experienced several dreams like that. Dreams where he would walk through endless malls and precincts without ever knowing how he had got there or where he might end up.

All the shops by now appeared to be closed. Beset by the prospect of still being there when the lights went out he was hurrying along a passage lined with smaller shops, all in darkness, when he spotted her standing outside one of them. She struck him at once as one of his own fictional characters – an image of the attractive young woman he had created as a main player in his novel! He was intrigued yet wholly relieved at finding another human being. She was attempting to fasten her bag when it slipped from her grasp to spill several of its contents onto the floor. As he approached, her lipstick rolled to his feet.

'Let me help you,' he offered, picking up the lipstick.

'Oh, you're very kind. It's only a few bits and pieces.'

'No problem, really. And, er – I'm a bit lost. You wouldn't happen to know the way out of this place, would you? I'm parked near the town square.'

'The town square? Yes – it's back along there. You're not far from the exit. I have to go out the other way but you can't miss it. And - really - you are very kind.'

'Er - look,' he began, convinced he could not simply walk away after this bizarre encounter, 'I feel completely out of order in asking and it - it, er, seems a bit pushy - but will you meet me here for lunch early next week? It's important but I really can't explain right now.'

Her green eyes were upon him. A smile dimpled her cheeks. Eternal seconds passed before she answered.

Once more alone, the spontaneity of his question continued to surprise him. He'd expected a sharp rebuff. Her answer had surprised him even more and as a result the world seemed altogether brighter as he stepped out into an evening of lowering cloud and chilling drizzle. As the iron gates clanged shut behind, he imagined he could still hear the tap-tap-tap of her high-heels receding along the otherwise deserted passage.

***

He visited the shopping centre a second time two days later. This time it thronged with chattering, late morning shoppers. Curious, he thought, how the memory can play tricks. The precinct no longer struck him as confusing or over large yet the passage where he was sure he had spotted the woman proved impossible to identify

51

with any certainty. Until their first lunchtime assignation the following week he began to take seriously the thought that his first visit to the centre, and his encounter with her, were an outpouring of his imagination; a vivid episode conjured up for inclusion in the novel. That night, sound asleep, he found himself strolling again in the empty precinct. This time he was afraid. Very afraid. Something watched unseen as he wandered in search of a way out. Just out of sight it waited.

***

Their table was bathed by the glow of a candle flame and the warmth of muted wall lights. She regarded him from over her glass of red wine. Dark-sheened hair caressed her cheek and flowed about her shoulders. Her gold earrings and pendant displayed small renaissance suns. Her perfume was an invisible mist of sensuality. Her dress of deep purple fabric was low cut and hugged her slim curves to just above the knee. He found her unnervingly glamorous and her voice, one he had come to think of as 'smoky,' held his full attention.

'I'm glad you agreed to meet me for lunch,' he said after polite formalities and his summary explanation as to why he had asked her. The ensuing silence made him edgy. Voices from other customers in the small bistro situated off the main concourse seemed now to intrude, to threaten a delicate situation.

At last she replied, 'Yes, Simon, it's less than a week since we met, isn't it.'

'Yes, less than a week,' he agreed. 'It's incredible how time can fool people; sitting here it seems like only hours, not days since then.'

'The way you propositioned me in the shopping centre,' she smiled. 'I thought that was rather sweet. And this book you mentioned; the one you're writing – it sounds so very interesting.'

'Well like I said, I felt I already knew you. Your name, Tamara – you said it's Russian. The girl in my book is called Tanya because her parents were Russian. I tell you it was a real shock, though all we're doing now is passing small talk. I know so little about you. You don't wear a ring. Are you -?'

'Married? No, I'm not married – and you?'

'Oh, I was once,' he breathed. Downing more of his wine he gazed into her eyes. 'She ended up with an estate agent – poor girl. But I'd rather not bore you with the details.'

'It's your novel I really want to know about,' she said leaning closer to him. 'What role does my look-alike, Tanya, play? Is she heroine or victim? I hope you don't plan on killing her off.'

'Er no, but well, it's all pretty spooky stuff, horror fiction actually. It's a situation where there's no barrier between fantasy and reality. Nightmares become real and the real world turns out to be an illusion. I haven't figured out the ending yet so whatever I say now might turn out not to be true. She will, of course, remain beautiful throughout but best if I e-mail the manuscript to you when it's finished – if it ever is. It's taken me over completely. Now and again I wake up at night thinking what's in the novel is real and wondering if what is real isn't, especially when it comes to shopping centres.'

'Then I'll have to wait until your book finished, won't I?'

Here was an opening. What he wanted to ask her had been anchored by caution during lunch but now it had to be said or there would be little point in his hoping to meet her again. 'Look, I – you're still something of a mystery to me but I'm at a loose end when it comes to personal relationships. I'll admit the fault is entirely mine since I get far too absorbed in my work. What I'm saying is, I'd like you to join me for dinner one evening next week. I'd be happy to drop you back home afterwards – if I had any idea where you live, that is. I've already told you where I'm based. But as you hardly know me I'll say nothing more if that's what you'd prefer. I hope you understand.'

'Of course I understand. I wouldn't play you along for a free lunch and I hope that's not the way it's seems.' She drank the remains of her wine then continued, 'I live a few miles out of town in the opposite direction to you but there's a place we could eat locally. I don't think you'd want to drive back late at night after drinking, though. I could put you up at my house for the evening. It's an old property only a short walk from the village. There's plenty of room.'

***

Her reply once again had surprised him. It was more than he would have dared hope for. He'd been tempted to smile but had not, fearing she might consider it an expression of conquest. Her parting kiss had been the first they had exchanged but it had been warm and passionate. As passionate as if they were already lovers. Driving home his mind was possessed anew by her words and by her image. The novel could wait.

It was Monday of the following week when he again visited the shopping centre. Because he had met her there and because it was there she had agreed to meet him later, he had come to regard the precinct as a venue of good fortune. He thought he recalled the location of the bistro where they had sat for lunch but it was no longer where he thought. Instead there was a cut-price shoe shop.

'Must be in another part,' he murmured to himself. 'Or maybe it changed hands over the weekend,' Units, he recalled, sometimes closed one day then reopened soon after in a different guise.

Nevertheless, he was greatly puzzled.

***

They were seated opposite one another in the candle-lit alcove of a small village pub and though wishing to avoid the banality of small talk he asked the inevitable, 'D'you come in here often?'

'I've never been here before,' she smiled. The casual black two-piece outfit, not too low cut, not too short, fitted her to perfection. Her lips were crimson red against the pale smoothness of her cheeks. Her eyelashes were long and dark. Her earrings, black flame opals set in gold filigree. She was too pure, too excellent an image for him to assess as mere flesh and blood.

'The food here is rather good,' she added, much to his relief.

'I think so, too,' he replied. 'But this pub is only a five-minute walk from your house. If it's your first time here, where d'you usually go?'

He really wanted to know if anyone else took her out to dinner or if she had a male partner.

'Oh, nowhere local,' she answered. 'I've never been a pub person. I try to avoid noise. I'm old-fashioned, you see. I have no television and no mobile phone.'

It pleased him that there was no intrusive rock music and no TV screen or fruit machine to disturb their evening and that the customers behaved as people ought to behave.

'And where you live,' he said, 'I take it the house is yours: It's pretty ancient from what I saw of it, and quite large. Hope you don't mind but I mooched around the hallway whilst you were upstairs. The wooden panelling looks Jacobean – maybe earlier. Is the house as old as that?'

She lingered over his question then answered, 'Yes, the house is very old. But it's warm and comfortable. It suits me for now.'

'And the cat – what's he, or she, called?'

'The cat?' Tamara peered at him quizzically. 'I don't have a cat.'

'But I glimpsed one before you came back down - I swear I did, though it was only for a moment. A large black cat. It was looking at me though the rails near the top of the stairs,'

'Simon, dear, it must be your writer's imagination. The stairs are not well lit as you saw. The shadows in that house can play tricks. I have no pets. I never have.'

He was tempted to insist there *had* been a large cat. A very large cat. But he did not wish to contradict her or to compromise what he hoped would develop into a sound relationship. Nor did he wish to jeopardise the possibilities of the night

56

ahead, if possibilities there were. He refilled their wine glasses and said nothing more about the cat.

'What about you?' she asked. 'You said you lived alone because of your work. Is that the way you prefer it or am I prying?' Her manner remained demure.

'No,' he smiled, 'you're not prying. Being an author is a solitary occupation. Distractions are the last thing you need. As I mentioned when we had lunch together, I'm better off left alone when I'm working. There have been times when I could have spent a month or so in some remote lighthouse. No phone, no TV - just me, my laptop and a crate or two of red wine. But that doesn't mean I'm antisocial. I quite enjoy company when I'm not busy.'

'You don't strike me as a recluse, Simon. You must have friends. Surely you have people around to visit now and again otherwise you'd end up a hermit.'

'Ah, but that's exactly why I'm renting the apartment. My phone stays switched off most of the time. None of my friends know where I am and they won't until the book is finished. And as for being alone - far from it.' He sat upright and leaned closer to her. 'I'm surrounded by the characters in my novels day and night. I live their lives. I know their feelings. I speak their words because I have to - good and bad. They're all there waiting in the wings, all ready to step out and say or do their bit. Some of them are more real to me than a good many individuals I've encountered in the past. A lot of people find this difficult to understand. But, Tamara, I get the feeling you do understand.' He had come to regard her as a woman of intellectual depth. He preferred women like that – women like the main character of his book whose fate was yet to be determined.

Tamara sipped her wine and smiled, 'I understand perfectly. As you mentioned over lunch, the door between this world and that of the imagination is forever open to those with imagination.'

Simon relaxed back in his chair. 'I suppose in many ways it is, yes.'

'Are you not afraid of what might come through that door from the other side, especially when you're alone? Is that not where nightmares arise?'

He laughed self-consciously and replied, 'I certainly hope not but I have to believe in my characters or the reader wouldn't.'

'Yes, Simon, of course,' she smiled, 'but then they are as you say only fiction. And I have broken your spell of solitude.'

'Well I'm not about to complain,' he smiled back. 'But you live on your own as well, although you mentioned you did secretarial work. And that house of yours is a lot bigger than my apartment. I'd have thought you'd be the lonely one, except when you're out at the office. I assume you have company there – don't you?'

'No, I don't. My work is done on-line. It's all contract work. I don't see anyone at all.'

'God, Tamara, that makes you even more of a recluse than me – and at your age, with your looks. That's incredible. And that house of yours – has anyone suggested it might be haunted?' Once more in his thoughts prowled the cat.

'Haunted,' she replied. 'Yes, women tend to believe in that kind of thing more than men don't they. No, I have never seen a ghost in all the time I've lived there. I never believed in ghosts.'

'How long *have* you lived there,' he asked, sensing she was not inclined to discuss the matter of ghosts.

Before she was able to reply, the waiter, a sallow youth with an expression devoid of enthusiasm, sauntered over to their table. Collecting the plates, he reached across and almost knocked over her half full wineglass. His murmured apology was met by a wide-eyed glare as, switching her head about with teeth bared, she half rose from her chair and hissed in his face, 'You stupid fool!'

The waiter froze in startled consternation then hurried away whilst the mask of anger vanished from Tamara as quickly as it had appeared. Mildly shocked, Simon kept silent. When she spoke again it was as if the incident had never happened. 'Shall we go soon?' she asked. 'It's getting late.'

***

'Sorry I couldn't offer you parking space,' she said as they strolled along the deserted village street.

'That's no problem,' he responded. 'The public car park is free at night, anyway.'

The night was cold with rain threatening. The expression on her face, the sound of her voice in response to the waiter's misdemeanour - both had left a profoundly disturbing impression on him. But when she linked her arm reassuringly into his, when he felt her warmth, when he breathed her perfume, the affair seemed unimportant. At the solid oak front door she withdrew an iron key from her bag and turned to brush fingers with hot feather touch down his cheek. 'Simon, dear, do you still want to stay here tonight?'

'What d'you think? Of course I do – unless you've changed your mind.'

'Oh, no, I haven't changed my mind.'

The door swung in with a sigh. They entered the dimly lit hallway where his small suitcase had been left. He was about to ask where he was to sleep when she slipped her arms about him. Her gaze was intense, her breath a furnace of sensuality. 'Simon - you'd like to share my bed, wouldn't you?'

'Share your -' He drew breath before murmuring, 'Christ, yes.'

Their lips met with a passion that fired him, with an intensity that devoured free will yet offered the prospect of untold pleasures. Slipping off her coat she moved to the stairs and swung about to face him. 'Give me ten minutes. My door will be ajar. The bathroom is at the far end of the landing. And, Simon, only use the bathroom light. The wiring upstairs needs to be looked at.'

He watched her ascend into semi-darkness, glanced at his watch then waited in anticipation, aware in the silence of his own heartbeat. A door opened and closed. Water was running. Floorboards creaked above. In the half-light he peered about to scrutinise linen-fold wood panelling, time-chewed wooden beams and doorframes rendered askew by the burden of centuries. This was not the house of a young and beautiful woman. It was more a museum that exuded discreet vapours of a vanished age. And though well kept, it seemed to him devoid of any lived-in feeling. There were no pictures on the walls, no ornaments. Perhaps she considered the panelling rendered them unnecessary.

How long had she lived here? She had never replied when he asked her in the restaurant and he had not thought to ask a second time. In the heavy silence his attention drifted to the landing above where on that first occasion he had seen, or imagined he had seen, the cat. There was nothing other than the darkness that prevailed. He wondered if she really did live alone in so large a house. Then the thought occurred; did she entertain other men as readily as she now proposed to entertain him? Was it her business? Was it the real source of her income? No, they had spent enough time together and there had been no mention, no hint of a transaction. He could no longer regard her as a conquest because the situation was by now more her making than his. Alerted by a creak from above, he glanced at his watch.

The allotted ten minutes had passed.

Climbing the stairs he found himself in near darkness until entering the bathroom. The brass and white ceramic Victorian accoutrements appeared in good order. There were towels and there was ample hot water yet the room lacked those bottles and jars that served female demands. Leaving his clothes folded outside the bathroom door he switched off the light then made his way along the landing. On entering the bedroom it took some time for his eyes to adjust, some time before he could make out her naked figure standing by the heavily curtained window.

***

Their lovemaking had been as passionate, as spontaneous as ever he had desired, as ever he had known or imagined he might ever know. The old bed, a brocade-curtained four-poster, had served as a temple of voluptuous pleasure and afterwards as a refuge of sleep and comfort.

He awoke within a well of blackness. There was no sound. But there was fear. He breathed in deeply, wondering what the time was, wondering why he felt so afraid. The aftermath of a nightmare, perhaps? Yes, it must have been a nightmare - but he had no recollection dreaming. His watch rested on a small cabinet just outside the brocade to his right. The dial was luminous and, if he could reach out to find it without disturbing her, he would know the time. He did not reach out but remained staring into darkness, reluctant to move yet wishing he was far away, back alone in his apartment. He would try to sleep, try to remain as he was until daylight filtered through the curtains beyond. But the brocade – that would need to be opened or he would not see any light. He eased up on the pillow to shift the brocade aside, only to feel the heavy material drop back again.

A glow appeared to his left. He turned aside to find two eyes staring at him not an arm's length away. Two green eyes. Eyes with wide-open black slits.

'God!' he cried. 'That bloody cat!' He reached out to shake her, calling, 'Wake up! Wake up will you!' But his hand fell upon fur, warm fur that

moved by his side even as the eyes moved. 'No –
no!' he shouted as the eyes widened, as the mouth
snarled, as she began to rise from the bed. Then the
voice – a low, moaning that arose louder as the
words came. 'Sssstay – sssstay here with me!'

He tumbled aside with a cry, wrenched at the
brocade, felt her breath on his neck, felt the piercing
sharpness of claws on his shoulder as he fell out
onto the carpet. 'No!' he cried again, scrambling,
reeling across the room amidst darkness to where he
hoped the door would be. 'No! No! No!' He was
cold with fear as his fingers grasped the handle.
Hair bristled on his neck. He fled the room to
collide with the banister opposite. In mindless terror
he blundered naked along the landing to the top of
the stairs fearful of looking back. But there was
light! Light from below where in the hallway a
small lamp still glowed. He plunged down the
stairs, almost sprawling headlong at the bottom
before he regained sufficient balance to reach the
front door. He tugged and twisted the handle but the
door was locked. Spinning about, he glimpsed the
cat on the landing, green eyes fixed upon him
through the banister rails as it loped purposefully to
the top of the stairs. Seized by panic he dashed to
the first door along the hallway. The door flew
inward but before closing it behind, he glimpsed
another door on the far side of the room and once
more in darkness blundered on, colliding noisily
with he knew not what until reaching it. Beyond this
door the wavering glow from an iron fire grate
illuminated a small, heavily furnished room with no
windows and in moments he was hastening through
a third door to his right.

His heart pounded, his breath came in gasps. He stopped with his back to the door and for infinite moments was unable to move. The low moan of a cat sounded from the other side. Raw fear was his master and making out yet another door he headed the only way he could, stumbling, striking furniture, knowing the great cat followed with silent step.

Soon he must find his way from the house. Soon one of the doors must open into the night, into freedom. But one room led to another, all in near darkness, then another in this impossible nightmare maze until despair overtook him. He fell gasping against the next door because it was locked. Across the room through which he had just passed he heard the handle of the door turn.

'Oh, God, let me out! Let me out! The glacial hand of fear gripped ever tighter - a fear that rendered him incapable of thought or action. A dark form loomed as he spun through a howling void of insanity.

Something touched his shoulder. He screamed.

'Steady on, sir,' came a voice from beyond. 'Steady on!'

'W-what!'

'Calm down, sir, you've had a panic attack. Calm down and I'll see if the house doctor is still around.'

His eyes started fearful wide. He gazed uncomprehending. Stared about to find himself collapsed and cowering in the doorway of a darkened shop. The hand resting on his shoulder belonged to a figure in black uniform that bore a yellow security badge. Drawing a deep breath, he glanced in disbelief at the man then up at bright lights in the arcade ceiling.

'Take a few deep breaths, sir,' said the man. 'Stay where you are while I get on the phone,'

'Wait – no, don't call anyone! Wait, I - I'll be all right.'

'You're shaking like a leaf, white as a sheet and cold as ice. Looks like you need medical assistance.'

'N-no, give me five minutes. Just five minutes and I'll be OK. I just need time to think, that's all. Just a few more minutes - please.'

'Afraid we can't wait, sir, unless it's an emergency. The shopping centre is closed now and I've to lock the main gates. What about a taxi to take you home? We can call one from here. Got enough cash for a cab, have you, sir?'

'No – I mean, yes,' he stammered, struggling to his feet. 'I've got cash, but I don't need a cab. Just - just show me the way out. I'll be fine as soon as I'm outside. I – I need fresh air.'

'Turn right at the end, sir, and you'll see the exit directly ahead. Gate's still open.'

'Please – show me yourself. I want you to actually take me out of here.' Then gripping the door frame to steady himself he added, 'Please, that's all I need.'

'No problem, sir - I'm going there anyway and I'll hold you steady.'

As they approached the gate Simon hesitated. 'Look – I'm sorry if I've caused problems when you're trying to lock up. It's the first time anything like this has happened. I can't explain -.'

'Not to worry, sir,' assured the security man, gripping his arm as though wishing to hasten his departure. They reached the gate and the security man said, 'Now you go straight on home.'

'Yes, I'll do that. My car's not far away. Look, thanks again. I'm really sorry for all the fuss.'

The security man, sliding bolts shut, peered at him through the bars. 'Never mind, sir – someone has to be last out.' Then glancing over his shoulder he added, 'Except for that ruddy black cat heading our way. Still, it can squeeze through the bars whenever it wants.'

He turned around and began, 'Hope you soon feel -' then as the cat slipped by, added. 'Blimey, he's shot off like a champion sprinter!'

Nightmare

Her hands rested loosely folded across her lap whilst turquoise lights danced in her eyes. Glowing butterflies that circled one about the other. The lights were all she saw. From somewhere beyond flowed his words, soft and reassuring. 'Relax.'

'Yes,' she answered, 'I'll relax.'

'You are warm and comfortable. Warm and very comfortable.' The voice came from a distant place, from another time. 'Your eyes are heavy and you wish to sleep. You are drifting into sleep.'

Her eyes closed, her mouth opened slightly. It was so much easier now than in those desperate days when she had first come to him.

'Do you hear my voice clearly?'

'Yes.'

'How do you feel?'

'Warm. Warm and safe.'

He eased his chair a little closer. 'We are going back into your dream. You feel you can do that once more, don't you?'

A frown crossed her face and she whispered, 'I - I don't know.'

'No one will make you do it but you have done so well. You have been so brave.'

Her expression became peaceful but only for a time.

'Will you try once more? Please try. Once you are through you will be free of anguish and fear. This will be your final journey – a journey into freedom.'

Catching her breath she whispered, 'He always said he would come back for me whatever happened. Even after death. Always he used to say that. He must never come back again.'

'Relax. He can never come back in the real world. You are quite safe.' Leaning closer, he watched the tension ease from her face then added, 'As strong as he was, as much as you fear him in your dreams, you are winning. You have the strength to complete the journey. Tell me you will do it.'

Her lips barely moved, 'Yes, I will do it.'

***

She stood where she had found herself often before in that bleak place, gazing out from a headland that swept down to a leaden sea. A sea that rose and fell with dead-eye sheen under a chill, grey sky. To her left, bare rock sloped upward to what she knew must be a precipice of fearful aspect, though she had never dared approach the edge. Only short, terrifying steps to her right the stony ground ended, plunging vertically to form one side of a deep inlet bounded by black cliffs. Beckoning in cavernous horror, it drew her gaze as it threatened to draw her body and soul. Within this well of annihilation, water growled in mockery of life and hope.

Had the sun ever shone here? Had it ever brought warmth to this grim realm? The breeze disarrayed her hair. Icy spray drove up from far below to sting her cheek. Ragged clouds advanced above the water - pallid fingers that grasped the air, tearing apart then reforming.

Turning away, she started along rough ground. The anguished turmoil of the sea faded and she was conscious of her own breathing and the grating of bare stones under her shoes. Some way ahead arose a rock wall, bone-pale against the barren sky. Before its base lay tilted slabs, exposed to the elements in jagged disarray. Threatening forms that crowded in upon the path she had to take. Once, she remembered, she had stopped here not daring to go further. It might have been yesterday. It might have been a lifetime ago. The path disappeared amidst looming stone sentinels but she went on, finding her way around and through, until she stood before the entrance to the cave. There a narrow archway leered in petrified gape - the twisted snarl of an overthrown giant.

At the entrance she stopped to turn and face back the way she had come. Through the chaos of slabs she could still make out the sea. The sky was darkening now, the torn clouds thickening, lowering, reaching down to draw away her warmth and her spirit. Arms folded across her chest against the cold, she walked on, passing beneath the arch, the tread of her feet on loose stones answered by a mocking echo from within - a ringing, hollow cackle.

After a time, walking became easier, the ground quite even and largely free of loose stones. She no longer needed to reach out to maintain her balance. The walls were smoother and lighter and the rough cave had become a curving gallery with no visible end. In the still air hung a timeless, cathedral-crypt odour. The gallery should have been dark but was not. All about, a dim light pervaded the walls, having no visible source, casting no shadow. She had wondered about the light. Wondered but never believed there could be an answer. Those same walls slanted here inwards, there outwards, sometimes bulging as a great stone belly that she feared might split open and collapse to crush her.

Pressing on deeper, one arm raised, she was aware of diffused marks, odd, random patterns in muted colours that had begun to appear about the walls. In the echoing stillness, her breathing came louder. Louder as if someone or something crouched nearby, breathing with her - perhaps out of sight around the next bend, perhaps stalking quietly behind. A bear-like form waiting to rise from the shadows. Always before, always when passing through, the fear had assailed her, but no two journeys would be quite the same. Nothing could be certain. Nothing except that which she most dreaded. Above the beating of her heart she whispered, 'I won't turn back now - whatever happens – I won't.'

Writhing over grey walls, the amorphous discolorations appeared now less diffused. They had begun to acquire tantalising forms. She could not have said at which point any of them became recognisable images because even the most random and ill-defined of patterns might occasionally suggest something familiar. Often she had gazed up at the clouds on a placid day, sometimes into the embers of a dying fire to discover forms and faces. Further on and she perceived the markings on the gallery walls to have attained a semblance of living things. Featureless, still, but suggestive of dwarf-like figures standing, crouching, jumping or running. She fixed her gaze ahead, wanting to ignore them, but there was always another corner, always another bulging wall to intensify her fears.

In less than a dozen hollow steps the once uncertain forms suggested images of people with crudely defined limbs, heads, and soon, a semblance of faces. She began to hurry. Almost stumbling in her haste she tried to ignore the images. After another twist in the gallery she stopped, wide-eyed and anxious. Here were people she knew, blurred like watercolours applied to wet plaster. People from her past. She reached out to them with trembling hand but dared not touch. Eyes fixed upon the ground she carried on but with each convolution of the passage the figures grew to demand attention. Ever more real and pressing closer. Pressing closer because the gallery had imperceptibly narrowed.

Again she stopped, for she was close to another threshold, a place where once before she had found reason crushed by fear. But determination still burned bright and she forced herself on. From the corner of her eye she noticed the figures beginning to move. Imperceptibly at first then in silent, fluid motion, staring from the walls with a blank gaze. Staring to infinity as ancient votary figures.

At the next turn there was no question of pressing on for the figure spreading slowly across the curved wall was that of her younger self. More real than the other forms, the eyes were alive and she was smiling. The image stood in blue school uniform with brown leather shoulder bag. Stood alone, as if waiting for someone. If only that silent image - the person she once had been - if only her younger self had understood. Here she was tempted to stay a while.

On again and there were her parents, her school friends and her first teenage date. She sat before the small mirror in her room, putting on lipstick, perhaps for the first time. The vivid red lipstick of which her parents had so disapproved. Reflected in the mirror, the eyes of the image, looked directly at her. She wanted to speak to her innocent, to her so naive bygone self - to call back through time with a warning. Had her past self ever imagined other eyes watching from the shadows and thought it no more than a trick of the light?

The years replayed in silent, slow motion and she hesitated once more. Here she was, a young woman, slim and vivacious, her schoolgirl image cast off as surely as had been the uniform. Here were more friends and acquaintances, some old, some new. Once more her parents and -. A veil of sorrow descended. Here was the fair-haired young man who once desired her more than she desired him. The one she had rejected in favour of another. The one to whom she might have turned for real and lasting affection. The one whose life had ended so tragically. Ended even as the shadow of another was falling across her path.

The silent parade drifted inexorably by. People, once a part of her life, some she had known well, some she could hardly recall. She watched their mouths open and close, eyes turning one to the other, some stern, some happy, some laughing, their images flowing, expanding and diminishing about contorted stone.

Another turn and she faltered. This image loomed still and alone. A steel-blue gaze fell upon her. He stood as she remembered when they first met, cocky and confident, shirt half-undone to display those gaudy tattoos, hands thrust into pockets, hair unkempt - his stubbled jaw set in a deceptive grin.

She moved on, pressing as close to the wall opposite the image as she could, knowing the eyes were hard upon her as they had been in those early days. A distant voice - a whispering - an echo from a dream urged her on. She knew what must come next but she could not continue without looking up.

She was with him in this phantom world, making love, laughing, dancing, drinking. Watching with amusement that quickly turned to anguish as he confronted another in one of his drunken brawls. She saw herself on the doorstep and in tears, refusing to meet him again. Saw herself in the end, as always, giving in; helping him when he was broke, helping him when he was drunk, sick and disgusting whilst others looked away, ashamed. Always there was the making up and the physical passion when they were alone. A physical passion that blossomed so dark and so wide as to obscure from her a truth the world could plainly see.

About her drifted other voices, mingled and indistinct, echoing with her own thoughts to nurture the illusion of this other world. Like the sombre clouds at the beginning of her journey, the figures merged, formed, reformed. Here was the wedding – her wedding. She watched her parents smiling with the crowd then standing aside to look at each other in pained doubt. There were his parents, relatives and friends raising beer glasses, some looking ill at ease in more formal attire, some never having taken the trouble, several drinking too much, only to relinquish all pretence of dignity. Some becoming foolish, incoherent and abusive. Herself once again, cheerfully dismissive yet inwardly embarrassed.

The scenes passed in tormenting detail. Their private life flickered over the walls and she saw them together in newly established domesticity. She recalled the excuses she had contrived to offer her parents and friends when already her cherished illusions had begun to wither on the ill-nourished vine of hope. She recalled his increasing indifference, his intolerance and scorning of her friends and family, his excessive drinking and loutish manners.

The scenes resolved with fewer people. The tide of voices ebbed away. There remained only the two of them. She saw herself hurt and crying whilst his voice rose in anger and his violence fell upon her. A tattooed arm flashed before her eyes as his fist raised up to strike. She flinched, cowered against harsh rock, expecting the blow to fall. The gallery encroached, suffocating, terrifying. His voice rang about the walls in foul abuse. Hands clasped to her ears she sobbed and started to run but his image loomed at each turn, rising like an angry beast, raging, threatening until she cried out in despair!

Suddenly, he was gone. A faint echo retreated as clattering pebbles through the gallery, then - silence. She rested with hands and forehead against cold, now featureless stone, her cheeks wet with tears. After a while she turned, wondering if the torment could at last be ended and freedom within reach. But it was not ended. She admitted to herself it was not and realised she was soon to be confronted by the memory she dreaded above all others.

More images. As real in her thoughts as they were upon the cavern walls. They had argued and she had threatened to leave him as she had threatened so often before. Again he had abused her, physically as well as verbally. He had knocked her violently aside, pounded up the stairs to their bedroom where she had followed to watch through the open door. Watched in cold fear as he seized and pocketed her mobile phone from the dressing table, wrenched out the drawer containing her most treasured possessions. Watched tearful as in mindless anger he had crushed under his boots those small keepsakes she had cherished over the years. Those belongings that were a thread through the dark labyrinth to happier times.

At the next turn, another, larger image flowed over the gallery wall. It began to resolve in detail and it made her heart pound because it portrayed that which no one must discover. It was here terror had triumphed. It was at this very spot she had turned back to flee the way she had come. To where she could not recall except that she had stumbled in sightless panic then floated in black emptiness for a long time. Here was the truck - the old blue truck he used for odd-jobbing and who knew what else. He was working underneath exactly as she remembered on that day. She watched herself drift in silence, into the picture. Watched herself stand close and gaze down as his legs, protruding from beneath the engine, shuffled and flexed. And whilst the tears were gone, her eyes were still reddened, her face still bruised, her hair unkempt. Her expression spoke of emptiness. It said nothing mattered any more. Her image moved as if through deep water to stoop and twist the handle of the jack. She and her image were as one. Both watched the truck descend in silence though in her mind his screams pierced like burning steel before upwelling blood and thick-oiled metal quenched them. His feet kicked wildly then fell still as blood spread from beneath the truck to glisten bright against the asphalt. Slowly, the image blurred and faded from the walls and she walked away as dazed as she had been when she walked from the truck on that terrible day. It had been so very easy.

They had tried to hold her back when the truck was lifted but to no avail. She had gazed, stomach churning, upon the cratered chest, upon bloodied, staring eyes and red jaws that grinned impossibly wide. She had to know he was truly dead. They had offered consolation, of course, not recognising in her tears an outpouring of thankful relief.

The passage grew dimmer, walking became more difficult as she clambered over uneven ground, hands pressed against cold walls to keep her balance. It was becoming dark but the air stirred. A soft breeze whispered fields, flowers and open skies. Around the next turn diffused light picked out leaning walls and fallen rubble. She stumbled onward, turned one last bend then saw blue sky framed in a high arch. Below the entrance, ferns and bushes glowed in sunlight.

She emerged into the warmth of a spring day. A day of bright innocence. A day of good fortune. The birds spun trinkets of sound that mingled in clear air above the scent of flowers. A lazy drone of insects, a welcome aroma of fresh grass made her feel this was the morning of a new world. A grassy tract stretched ahead to a gentle rise, whilst not far away at either side lay shaded woodland. She walked on, savouring the breeze and caress of the sun but feeling now a little tired - then, a little more. There was a young tree. Somewhere to sit and rest. A place to look at the sky and flowers and listen to the birds. Sitting on the grass, she leaned back against the trunk, hands resting loosely folded across her lap. So warm now. So comfortable. Two butterflies flashed like coloured jewels against the sky as her eyes closed. Glittering turquoise lights.

***

A voice touched her ear. 'You will soon be awake, and when you wake up you will be relaxed and happy. You will have no fear. No anxiety.'

The bird songs, the blue sky, the sun were gone, but the fragrance of grass still lingered

'Wake up and relax.'

He eased back his chair as her eyes opened. Confronted by a reality that seemed unreal she raised a hand to her forehead whilst her other gripped the edge of the couch. 'How long was I -?'

'Asleep? Not very long.'

'Oh, it was so good there. So pleasant in the warm sun.'

'It must have seemed a long time. How are you feeling now?'

She waited as fragments of memory assembled. 'I feel much better than before. Much better now that I -.' She hesitated, recalling now that final scene in the gallery.

'Coffee?' he asked.

'Yes please. A cup of coffee would be nice.'

Seated before his desk she asked him, 'Did I talk? Did I speak about what was happening?'

'Hardly a word,' he replied casually.

'Did I talk about -?' she hesitated. 'Did I say anything near the end, before I found the way through?'

'No, nothing,' he answered. 'And now it's all over.'

She watched his face, intently.

'You're on the mend,' he said, thumbing through his desk diary, 'and that's all that matters.'

'What about the nightmares? You said once I'd got through, they would go away.'

He looked up, smiling reassurance. 'From now on you'll be less troubled. Eventually, not at all. Today you have overcome the worst. I have helped, of course - but never imagine for a moment that the real success here is due to anything other than your own determination to win through. All I have done throughout is to help you realise you had that strength. I hope you understand that.'

'You're very reassuring,' she smiled, sipping coffee.

Despite the trauma of her dreams, her smile had become warmer with each visit. He recalled, too, how her eyes remained fixed upon his a little longer each time she came to see him. She had become more than just a patient, though his thoughts remained unspoken.

'I'm simply telling you the truth,' he continued. 'Why should I not? You're young, attractive and have most of your life ahead to enjoy now this burden is slipping from you.'

'None of that seemed to matter until recently,' she sighed.

'Well,' he went on, 'doesn't that prove how your old self is bouncing back the way we planned? By the time your course is ended those nightmares will be a thing of the past. Come and see me - not so soon this time. In four weeks - on the ninth. At the same time if it suits you.'

'Yes, that's fine,' she said, rising from the chair, taking her coat from the stand and smiling at him once more. 'And thank you so much. So very much.'

***

Three weeks had passed when she telephoned to cancel the next and all future appointments. He harboured feelings of regret that weighed more heavily with the passing days. She was, or had been, his patient and it would not be proper to think of her otherwise. Nevertheless, sitting alone with his notes at the end of each day, he found himself wondering what had become of her.

Another four weeks had passed when he received a call from her general practitioner informing him of her attempted suicide.

***

He sat by the bedside and observed her face - pale, worn and frightened as it had been on that first visit to his office. For a time she appeared not to recognise him.

'Why didn't you come and talk to me?' he asked as she turned her head to look at him. 'Could I not have helped you?'

'There's nothing you or anyone can do,' she replied hoarsely, 'You wouldn't understand.'

'I'd like you to talk to me now I'm here. I'd like you to help me to understand - but I'll go away if you prefer.'

She did not reply but stared up at the ceiling. A nurse appeared at the door and said, 'She's still very weak. Perhaps you ought not to -.'

'Please,' came the voice from the bed, 'I'd rather he stayed. I don't feel so tired now.'

'A few minutes longer then,' agreed the nurse, closing the door.

Turning to him she said, 'I'm sorry this had to happen. You must think me so ungrateful after all the effort you put into sorting out my problems. I know you spent a lot more time than -. I wanted to come back but I was afraid you'd find out and - well, what can it matter now.' She closed her eyes then whispered, 'I - I killed him, you know.'

'Yes, I knew what happened before your sessions finished. It's not my place to pass judgement. I came here only to find out why you harmed yourself when things had gone so well.'

Her voice was weaker now but her words quite clear in the silence of the room.

'I was so happy when the nightmares went away. After I last saw you the dream returned now and then but I always found myself in that glade - in warm sunlight and peace.' She closed her eyes once more. 'Yes, it was wonderful - so wonderful I wanted to be there every night. It was so real I sometimes had no wish to come back. If I hadn't believed I was alone there I might never have -.' Her eyes opened wide and the look of fear he recalled on first meeting her had returned. 'I began to walk away from the glade and through the woods to hear the birds. I never wondered where the path might go but it didn't matter until -.' She stirred uneasily before continuing. 'It happened when I was amongst the trees. I - I heard something close by.' Reaching from under the bedclothes she placed a cold hand on his. 'At first I thought it was my imagination - nothing more. It happened twice again then next time I knew. Someone was watching me from amongst the trees. I decided not to go there again but I couldn't stop it happening. A few nights ago I saw something move. I tried to ignore it but I had to turn around and - Oh, God! He was there! He was coming out of the shadows! His eyes were red and staring and his jaw hung all bloody - the way it was when - when -.' She closed her eyes, released his hand, splayed fingers across her face. 'He was reaching out - trying to speak - walking toward me. I ran back to the glade but he was coming after me as the dream ended. Next time he -. Next time or the time after he'll reach me. He'll reach me before I wake up! I couldn't face it! No – never!'

Her eyes sprang wide. Stared into empty space. 'He'll never go away. Never! There's only one way I can escape him and that is through my own death.'

He reached out to clasp her hand, saying, 'That isn't true. Please believe me.'

She turned to him, her expression one of fearful resignation. 'He's just as real in that other world as he was in this. Like - like a worm eating through my soul.'

'You trusted me before did you not?' he asked

'Yes, I always trusted you. I didn't want to stop seeing you but – but I was afraid you would discover the truth.'

'Then we must continue further. We must exorcise this demon.'

'But how?' she sighed, her gaze fixed upon his. 'What more can you do?'

Leaning closer he said, 'Together we will succeed. Together we will destroy him. If you'll let me, I will enter with you into that other world. Together we will pass through the looking glass. Together we will complete what we began. As strong as he once was, the dream world is his final refuge. Once we have driven him from there he will be gone forever.'

'And you can be with me in the dream?'

'Yes. I'll be there to hold your hand as I hold it now. Whatever is left of him will see us together and know it cannot reach you. Despair will sweep it away like a dead leaf in the wind. It will fall into an abyss from which it can never return.'

'But how,' she breathed, 'how when it's no more than a dream? I don't understand.'

'How do we know which is the dream - the nightmare - and which the reality. Perhaps here and now is the dream and soon we'll leave it behind. Perhaps reality is that which you discovered at the end of your journey and which we are soon to possess for ourselves.'

His image stirred her memories as had those within the secret gallery. It seemed she had always known him. He was fair, like the young man of her past. Could he have been watching her in those dreams - or in dreams of his own? Perhaps he had tried to reach out but she had failed to understand. Perhaps she had failed to recognise him through the darkness cast by the one she so dreaded.

Where now might the dreaming end?

Feedback

I had not spoken with Lawrence for some weeks. Seeing the lights and seeing his white haired, tall, stooping figure busy inside the laboratory amidst those flickering screens, I had several times approached, hoping to discover what he was up to. On each occasion the outer door was locked with an, 'ACCESS FORBIDDEN,' sign glowing above. I'd once rapped on the door, forgetting that the place was insulated against extraneous sound. It was after all an acoustics research facility with the main section sealed off altogether. Even so I doubt he could have heard me or anyone else because of noise from the synthesisers and other equipment he was playing around with.

My own work and frequent lectures kept me out of circulation most weekdays, though I spent as much time as most in the canteen or at the bar. Lawrence had not been seen there, either. I should mention right now he was regarded as eccentric even in a world where eccentricity was considered almost a virtue. But to be thought of as eccentric by other eccentrics was something else.

He had to come and go from the sound lab, albeit at the oddest of hours, but if anyone ventured to engage him in conversation he responded in one of two ways, if he responded at all. Usually he would pass by deep in thought with the merest grunt of acknowledgement. Alternatively, he might react as if startled then hurry on as if some emergency called. For a man devoted to research into the nature of sound, Lawrence seldom employed it in the service of verbal communication. His disdain for smart phones was no secret.

At his occasional, and in those latter days much less frequent lectures, his unease in the presence of female students grew in direct proportion to their numbers. His voice became drier, his manner blandly impersonal. Always regarded as a misogynist, it was suggested by some that Lawrence was gay. I thought not. No, his aversion to women was not directly sexual, as I discovered on one of those rare occasions when he felt inclined to confide in me. It was on an oppressively dull afternoon of the kind that keeps most people indoors when I came across him seated out of the way on a bench in the university grounds.

'It's their voices, Don. That damned awful shrieking when they get excited. I tell you, it cuts through me like a knife! Even hearing them talk at a distance makes me feel uncomfortable.'

'Maybe that's because you're working with sound all day,' I offered. 'Those synthesisers and signal generators – maybe you're becoming sensitised, you know, suffering from some kind of aural overload. Why not give yourself a break? A few days, a week away from that laboratory wouldn't do any harm, would it?'

He looked at me as though wanting to express some rather delicate matter; the way a person might when confessing to the use of a suppository. He turned away and muttered something about his work not having that kind of effect at all, then he glanced back, adding sharply, 'Don, my researches are more important than any of you realise. Much more! You'll see!'

He had significant papers to his credit, mainly in the field of seismology. Some of his published work dealing with the modulation of pressure waves at Earth's core-mantle boundary and, in particular, his papers on the propagation of low frequency waves through the crust were highly regarded. And although not connected with my own area of studies, linguistics, I found his work very interesting.

As spring matured into an unusually fine summer, staff and students alike enjoyed the university gardens, many taking lunch on the grass rather than in the canteen. It was during one bright, sunny day in the grounds that I struck up a friendship with Helen. I'd first noticed her long copper-brown hair and dark eyes during my own lectures but though I'd been divorced over a year, I usually confined my socialising to other members of the staff and people of roughly my own age. It was she, however, who sought me out. I won't go into details other than to say that, despite an age gap of some sixteen years, we soon found each other's company pleasurable in more ways than one, so it was her company I sought and she mine whenever possible.

Lawrence hadn't figured large in my thoughts for some weeks when a colleague asked if I had any idea what he was up to. I had not, I replied, noting a degree of concern as the man said, 'I swear he spends his entire day and much of the night alone in that damned laboratory, and he won't let anyone else in the place. It's highly irregular.'

I was aware of that but as Helen had recently moved into my apartment she was accounting for a much bigger slice of my life and that had made me a happier man.

'Look,' insisted my colleague, 'some of us are worried about him. He won't discuss his work with anyone face to face and if he has a telephone or a mobile no one has his number, nor do we have an e-mail address. Don, you've been on friendly terms with him longer than most of us - could you pop around to his house to check if everything is OK? If one of us doesn't do something - well, I'm afraid the situation has already attracted attention at a higher level.'

I agreed I'd try to have a word with Lawrence, but I didn't need to go out of my way as things turned out. I was strolling in the grounds one warm evening with Helen. It was ten-fifteen with the stars shining bright when a tall, lank figure clutching a laptop came hurrying along the path toward us. He was oblivious to our presence and would have passed us by had I not called, 'Lawrence - hello!'

He stopped abruptly, a nearby lamp reflecting in his thick, round spectacles. 'Oh - Don, it's you. Please don't think me rude but I have work to do. Mustn't hang about.'

He ignored Helen completely and I released her hand, saying, 'Lawrence you old bugger, what have you been up to hiding away from everyone? People are asking questions.'

'Are they really,' he muttered. 'Want their money's worth out of me, do they?'

'Nobody has put it that way,' I continued, 'We're all curious about whatever's keeping you so busy in the lab and, well, concerned you might be overdoing things.'

He looked hard at me and muttered, 'Mmm, yes, my project.'

Helen ran her fingers across my back and under my arm, trying to tickle me. It didn't work, I'm not ticklish, but I knew she was doing it because Lawrence looked so grave and she wanted to make me laugh. I'm not sure if he noticed but he cleared his throat and said, 'Look, drop by for a drink after eight o'clock tomorrow if you're free.' He at last glanced at Helen, adding, 'or the evening after if you're – er, too busy.'

With that he strode off briskly into the darkness.

'See you tomorrow then!' I called after him.

'Can I come too?' whispered Helen, her breath tingling my ear.

'I'm not sure he'd be happy about that,' I replied.

'What a miserable old fart,' she grinned.

'No, it's not that,' I insisted. 'He's a clever and dedicated man. He always lived for his work, though why it's got even more of a grip on him now, I can't say.'

'He can't have any social life,' she said. 'Not even friends. I couldn't stick that.'

'You don't have to,' I answered, slipping an arm about her slim waist. 'Let's stroll over to the pub for a night-cap.'

***

It was gone eight thirty when I arrived at Lawrence's front gate. I'd had some last minute preparatory work to do for my lecture the following day and it had taken me longer than expected. Fortunately, his house was under ten minutes' walk from the university. I'd told Helen, however, to expect me in our favourite wine bar at around ten but I had no idea what Lawrence had in store for me that evening.

Mature, spreading trees threw long shadows across the lawn to the mock Tudor facade of the house. The place looked heavy and sombre in the afternoon sun and I couldn't help but notice the garden. He had always been an enthusiastic gardener but now it appeared overgrown and neglected.

He opened the front door and stood aside, his face set in a weak smile as I entered the hallway. The place smelled slightly musty as I followed him through to the rear of the house. The main room was comfortably furnished in a heavy old-fashioned way, untidy but not excessively so. He had a housekeeper, evidently, for he was the last person who would bother to dust the mantelpiece clock. There was, however, something that looked entirely out of place – but I'll return to that in a moment.

'Can I get you a drink?' he asked, pointing me toward one of the easy chairs.

'Oh, mmm, yes,' I said with uncharacteristic hesitation, wondering if he might have meant tea or coffee. 'A Scotch please,' I added when I caught a whiff and realised it was Scotch that Lawrence had already been drinking.

He plucked his own almost empty glass from the mantelpiece. 'With -?'

'With nothing,' I replied, 'I prefer it without pollutants.'

'A man after my own heart,' he muttered, stepping to the drinks cabinet.

As I mentioned, there was something out of keeping with that room. Against one wall, supported by metal racking, stood his hi-fi system. The kind of set-up I would have associated with a recording studio rather than a domestic environment. On a table beside it rested a pair of old-fashioned, vertical, open reel tape decks and an expensive looking desktop computer. To the other side of the rack stood a storage unit that I guessed must have contained at least five hundred compact discs, and on top of this, the flat drums of a kind I had seen in his laboratory that I knew contained reels of magnetic recording tape.

'I see you bring your work home,' I said, easing myself into the chair.

'Now and again,' he answered, handing over a glass as generously filled as his own before sitting to face me. It was then I noticed the cat, a long-haired tabby. It was curled up asleep on a rug by the large, empty, low-arched fireplace - quite oblivious to my intrusion.

'Didn't know you had a cat,' I commented. An odd remark, perhaps, since I had never passed beyond his front door until then. Lawrence swirled the amber drink as if to focus his thoughts. 'So,' I pressed as diplomatically as I could, 'what's the project you're so deeply involved in?'

Seconds went by and I began to wonder if he'd heard my question. Then he glanced up and said, 'You like music don't you, Don? Shall we listen to a little music?'

'Er, yes, fine by me,' I replied, thinking maybe he didn't intend to answer my question.

'D'you like the later romantics?' he asked, rising from the chair.

'Yes,' I replied, 'my tastes cover most periods. How about yourself?'

'Very much so,' he answered, stooping before his collection of disks. 'I have a fondness for the likes of Brahms, Schumann, Dvorak - especially Brahms, especially the chamber works. Woefully neglected, I feel. Such depth of expression. Then of course we have Debussy and Ravel.'

'What about more recent composers,' I ventured. 'What about Shostakovich? Surely in the string quartets and the later symphonies; there is considerable depth of expression.'

'I suppose you're right,' he frowned, returning to the chair and reaching once more for his glass, 'but it is harmony I look for and I find some of the works you mentioned utterly despairing.'

I was about to comment further when the music began to play. 'Debussy,' I smiled.

'Yes, the Arabesques, more palatable when one has company, and such exquisite sound from the keyboard. It's as if the piano had been re-discovered by him.'

Would we ever get to the point of our meeting, I wondered?

'Tell me,' he said, settling into his chair, 'what are people saying? I'm causing a stir, am I?'

'Well,' I replied, 'you can't really blame them. You've all but stopped your lectures. You shut yourself away in that laboratory morning and night – weekends, too, from what I gather. The committee was bound to ask what you're up to sooner or later. I'm certainly curious.'

'Hmmm,' was his response. He took another gulp. His glass was already half empty. He said nothing but stared down at his hands. I tried not to shuffle in my chair but I was much aware of the mantelpiece clock ticking away precious time. My precious time.

'I suppose I ought to discuss it with someone,' he sighed at last. 'Yes, I really ought now that things are -.' Then staring directly at me he went on, 'I expect you to keep anything I say you to yourself - for the time being at any rate. It's most important at this stage. Will you agree to that, Don?'

This was awkward. How could I agree when I had no idea what he was about to tell me. 'Lawrence,' I replied, whimsically, 'if it's something inappropriate or illegal, you'd better not say anything at all.'

'No, no,' he smiled, 'believe me, it's nothing of the sort. But I'm not yet at a stage where I can demonstrate anything convincing. That's why I've kept quiet about what I have so far discovered.'

'Discovered? Well, OK,' I assured him, 'if it's to do with your work then I certainly won't tell anyone. If they ask I'll say you're involved in an important line of research and need time to compile your papers. Does that seem close enough to the mark?'

'It will do for now,' he answered, then lapsed once more into pensive silence.

I could see over the garden through the leaded windows at the end of the room. The sun had set and flame reddened clouds daubed the evening sky. The sky, the room, the music, everything seemed reassuringly normal.

'See her?' said Lawrence, nodding toward the fireplace.

'What? The cat you mean?'

'Yes, the cat,' he answered. 'What do you think the cat is hearing?'

It was an odd question and I wondered if there was an obvious answer he expected me to have at hand. 'You and I talking?' I replied. 'And the music I suppose. I'm assured cats are listening even when they're asleep.'

'Quite so,' he replied, 'but what do you imagine she makes of this music for instance? What must it sound like to a cat?'

'Oh, I see what you mean. Well, I guess it must be a meaningless and disordered stream of noises - yes?' I felt I was treading on thin ice at this point and wondered if he was about to demonstrate that his cat, and perhaps cats in general, were perfectly attuned to the music of Debussy and heaven knew who else, before revealing the fact to the rest of the world.

'You're absolutely right,' he said, much to my relief. 'It must seem utterly meaningless to her, to all cats, and to a good few human beings not a million miles from here I'm sad to say.'

'Right,' I answered. 'So where does that leave us?'

'I think you would appreciate,' he continued, 'that even the most devoted of music lovers has initially to become attuned to the sounds of an instrument or an orchestra - yes?'

'Yes,' I agreed, 'like a decent wine, or Scotch. When you're first exposed to these things, you maybe don't get much out of them. You have to give yourself time. At least most of us do.'

'Time - time - time. But you could give the cat a hundred lifetimes and she would gain little or no more insight or understanding into anything than she possesses here and now. Why?'

'Well, obviously,' I answered, 'cats and most living creatures, apart from ourselves and the higher primates, don't have sufficient mental processing power. They don't need it. They run on instinct and on those evolved behavioural patterns that have served them well for millions of years.'

'Perhaps - but is not our response to music, to art generally, an emotional response?'

'Yes, to a certain extent,' I agreed, 'but our responses to these things must be influenced by our intellectual faculties and it could be argued that human emotional responses cover a far wider spectrum than those of any other living creature.'

'Ah!' he exclaimed. 'Now we are getting there - slowly, but we *are* getting there.'

'Are we?' I answered. 'I'm not altogether sure where I'm going.' But I knew the drink was going to my head.

'Let me refill our glasses,' he said rising from his chair and taking the half-full glass from my hand.

'Not too much,' I began, 'I'm supposed to be meeting -.' my voice petered out. He wasn't taking any notice and returned with both glasses even fuller than before.

'Well now,' he said, resuming his place in the chair, 'I think we agree that through our enhanced mental development we are able to understand and to appreciate aesthetically those things in life that are denied to other living creatures - no matter how highly evolved they may be in other areas.'

'You might,' I responded, 'find those who study marine mammals disagreeing with you.'

'They might well disagree,' he smiled, 'but we'll wait in vain for a dolphin to write down a single note of music.'

'Fine,' I responded, 'but they may be attuned and emotionally responsive to things on a different wavelength. Attuned in areas we would not understand at all.'

I thought I was about to corner him in his reasoning but Lawrence leaned toward me with eyes greatly enlarged behind those thick spectacles and in a low voice said, 'Exactly, dear boy. *Exactly*.' He hesitated only long enough to down a quarter of his whisky. 'It should not come as too much of a surprise then if I were to suggest that elsewhere in our environment there exists a form of communication which, to a human being, would have as little meaning as this music has to our little friend sleeping peacefully by the fireplace.'

'I don't know if I'd be surprised or not,' I answered. 'It would rather depend on what you mean.' From the corner of my eye, I saw the cat move. She arose slowly, arched her back then peered straight at me with wide yellow eyes. I hoped she was going to head my way as I have a fondness for cats and this one was most attractive. But no - she turned lazily around and settled back down on the rug to face the opposite direction. 'Not a bad life for some is it?' I remarked.

'Wouldn't suit me,' replied Lawrence.

'All right, what's the point you were about to make?'

'You are familiar with the nature of my work are you not?'

'Reasonably so,' I replied, 'though I haven't read any of your more detailed papers.'

'No, I wouldn't expect you to - though I have downloaded a number of your articles on the structure and relationship of languages. I found them most interesting.' He took another gulp of Scotch. I at last felt he might be getting to the point - until he spoke again. I concluded then he had veered away to something else entirely.

'The Earth, as you know, is far from being a dead lump of rock. It is alive with large-scale movements. Convective motions in the outer core give us our magnetic field - convection in the mantle drives plate movements that split continents, build mountain ranges and generate volcanoes. Everything moving and changing over the ages but frozen in time to us poor buggers because we pass our lives in the blink of a geological eye. I've often wondered if there isn't some consciousness existing on an altogether different time scale to ours. I imagine it sitting there, up in the sky, watching mountains rise and fall as the continents shift around. Seeing the ice-caps flicker back and forth over the land as glaciers come and go like searching fingers. It probably wouldn't have noticed us yet. It might shift around eventually because its arse itches and pause to give itself a quick, thousand-year scratch. Then - fssst! We'd be gone.'

'Some people call it God - some call it Gaia,' I put in.

'Oh, yes, Gaia, seeing the planet as some kind of giant, self-regulating organism. Well that's one way of looking at things.'

Lawrence downed the remainder of his drink then looked at my glass to see if it needed refilling. It was still over half full so he did not embark upon another visit to the drinks cabinet. We discussed, albeit briefly, the merits, or not, of the Gaia hypothesis. When he returned to his intended theme I tried to suppress a sigh of relief.

'The crust of our planet is alive with oscillations, vibrations - sound if you like. When there's a major quake off Japan, Indonesia or the western Americas, the crust rings like a bell. Of course, the human ear is not attuned to these planetary twitches - we need instruments to detect and record them - unless we are unfortunate enough to have one occur under our feet.'

It was twilight outside now. I wondered if I might end up late meeting Helen and fingered the phone in my shirt pocket. But I didn't feel it appropriate to cut him short or use my mobile phone and risk wasting this rare opportunity.

'Early last year,' he continued, 'I began a programme of research with our newly updated computer facilities. I set out to build up a more detailed picture of crustal oscillations on a global scale. I expected everything to fit in nicely with the major tectonic patterns - which to a great extent they did. But I discovered something else, Don. Something absolutely unexpected.'

He leaned close to me once again, his eyes animated in a manner I had seldom witnessed. 'There are undercurrents. For a time I convinced myself these must relate to tidal movements, shifting faults, even avalanches - perhaps mining, oil drilling, even military operations. Some of them did, yes - but not all of them.' Adjusting his spectacles he announced gravely, 'Don, I believe I have discovered something of profound significance.'

'What have you discovered?' I asked.

'Coherent patterns,' he replied.

'Coherent? What d'you mean, coherent?'

'I mean some of the localised oscillations, the higher frequency ones; they don't relate to earth movements at all. But they appear, as I say, to be coherent.'

'Man made, you're saying - industrial?'

'No, dear chap, not man made at all. Not of human origin.'

I remained silent.

'There are discrete patterns. Yes, patterns. Not just in amplitude but in intervals and frequency shifts. I know you read Assyrian cuneiform, which to me as well as most people would be quite unintelligible. I would, however, expect to recognise repeating characters and groups. I would know it was a language without understanding a word of it. Don - *that* is what I have discovered.'

'Surely,' I said, 'these patterns have a logical explanation. You above all would see that.'

'Yes, that is what I thought. Exactly that - until I studied the phenomenon further. I have taken sophisticated recording equipment with me at weekends, miles away from here and in opposite directions. The same patterns occur. Wherever I look, they're there. Not all the time - they come and go, advancing, receding, passing to and fro in shifting sequences. It's like – it's like listening to a dialogue between -.'

'Between who?' I cut in as he hesitated. 'What kind of dialogue?'

'That's just it!' he exclaimed, raising his hands. 'I don't know - who - or what. But I tell you now - I intend to find out – and soon!'

'So why has nobody stumbled on this before?'

'Why? Why should they? Anyway, someone had to be first. And without the kind of equipment at my disposal, such phenomena would be impossible to detect, let alone analyse. It's the same with neutrinos or the cosmic microwave background. They've been there all the time but we never knew about them until science and technology gave us eyes to see.' He relaxed back in the chair and went on, 'A short time ago I discovered something else. It dawned on me whilst I was out making tests in the woods north of the reservoir. The wind was blowing - gusting through the trees above me. When I ran the data through that evening I realised that certain patterns tended to occur when the weather was active, others when it was calm.'

'Then surely, that's what it could be,' I said, 'some kind of feedback from the weather - pressure variations, electrical currents generated in the ground. Induction of some sort.'

'No, no, no!' he replied angrily. 'Don, you really are missing the point. The patterns are far too complex, too regular to be accounted for by such events. Once these patterns are computer processed and isolated from the general background mishmash I have no doubt whatsoever - there is a consciousness all about and beneath us. Believe me! Just what it is remains to be seen but I can assure you of that and of something else - something so amazing I found it hard to come to terms with at first. Don - it responds!'

'Responds?' I repeated the word, trying not to sound incredulous. By now, I had developed considerable unease over the direction our conversation had taken. If the high-ups in the university heard him talking like this his position might be in jeopardy.

'A while back in the lab,' he continued, his eyes bright, 'I took a recorded sequence and cleaned it up. It wasn't too difficult later on to run it through the amp into a transducer coupled to an outside, load-bearing wall. The university foundations are on bedrock so the sequence went straight into the ground from where it came. I switched on my recording gear and waited. D'you know what? There was nothing. Total, absolute silence.' Clasping fingers together beneath his chin, he rocked slowly back and forth. 'That, Don - that was what amazed me because it was the first time it had happened. It was like being in a room full of noisy, chattering people. You drop something that makes a crash or you call out and everyone goes quiet. Do you understand what I'm saying? That's what I did. I entered the room and shouted! And it worked! There *is* something and it knows. By God - it knows!'

I wondered how much he'd had to drink before I arrived, but no, it wasn't the drink. He was *very* serious and he was, after all, a leading authority in his discipline.

'Well, Lawrence,' I said at last, 'you're the expert. But honestly, to suggest there is some kind of all-pervading consciousness we don't know about sounds like you're out to start another religion and that's the last thing the world needs. We've had more than enough trouble over the centuries with the old ones and it's far from over.'

'Ah, yes - religion,' he responded. 'There may well be something in what you say. When I spoke earlier about my being the first to detect this phenomenon, I was thinking of modern times and scientific methods. In your study of ancient languages, which comprise a high percentage of religious and ritual texts - you must have encountered material relating to subterranean deities. Mythology is full of them from Egypt, Babylonia, Minoan Crete, China and the Americas. Isn't that so?'

'True enough,' I replied, 'but ancient peoples had deities for just about everything. It was their way of explaining natural phenomena. It was the *only* way they had. Today we have scientific evidence, even if some people choose to ignore it.'

'Quite so, but that in no way alters my findings. I am convinced that those ancient peoples must have had some inkling of this – this, whatever it is. After all, they were much closer to nature than we are. They didn't have our distractions. Life for them was a lot simpler.'

'So where do you go from here? What's your next move?'

'Hmm. I've had a few sleepless nights thinking about that, Don - believe me, I have.'

He spent a while in thought, twiddling the empty glass in his fingers whilst I glanced at the clock. In spite of such bizarre revelations I was concerned about my rendezvous with Helen. Even so, I didn't want to give the impression I wasn't taking him seriously.

'Are you staying for another Scotch,' he asked, 'or do you have somewhere else to go?'

'Well, since you mention it,' I replied, 'I'd arranged to meet up with Helen at ten o'clock and it's quite a walk from here.'

'Oh, that girl - yes. She's rather young isn't she, Don? Don't you think you should be a little cautious?'

'Not really,' I responded. 'She's old enough to decide for herself and I assure you she didn't need coercing.' With that I arose from the chair adding, 'Lawrence, I'd like to discuss this with you further. I think we should, you know, before it gets too involved.'

He walked ahead of me to the front door and opened it saying, 'Next time we meet I intend to have moved things along a bit.' I hesitated to see if he would elaborate but all he said was, 'I still take it, Don, that you will not discuss this with anyone? Please.'

'No, I won't. But I think you ought to get others involved, if only to validate your findings. Won't you consider doing that?'

'Goodnight, Don,' he said quietly, closing the door.

Outside the gate I tried to contact Helen on her mobile. There was no reply.

***

'I thought I'd been stood up,' she smiled, reaching to give my hand a squeeze.

'I'm not *that* late, am I? But I did try to phone you.'

'Oh, my mobile's buried in my bag – I often don't hear it. Look, there's a seat free in that alcove. I'll grab it. Mine's a vodka and lime by the way. No ice.'

She looked beautiful as ever - very glamorous in her short black dress and high heels.

'So how is the dry old stick?' she asked once I was seated.

'I'm not entirely sure.'

'Not sure! You've been chatting with him half the evening. What has he been up to all this time? Don, you have to tell me. The suspense is too much!'

'He made me promise not to discuss it, I'm afraid - but I don't know what to do, Helen, I really don't. Sitting in here with all these people around, with music playing, you wouldn't think that -.'

'Wouldn't think, what?'

'Well – well the poor old bugger's either blown a circuit or he's on to something very odd, I can tell you - or I can't, I mean. Not yet.'

'Go on, dearest,' she pouted, brushing lips against my ear whilst easing her fingers inside my shirt, 'give me a teeny-weeny hint.'

'Now, stop it!' I insisted, and changed the subject.

However it wasn't long before Lawrence was in the news, but not in the way I or anyone else could ever have anticipated.

***

Three days had passed when I returned from a conference in London. I arrived on campus not long after four o'clock. There'd been one of those electrical storms that clears the air after a hot, sultry day. The sky was beginning to brighten as I drove into the main car park but I realised it must have been quite a downpour because there were pools of water everywhere.

As I drew closer I saw an ambulance and police car at the entrance to D block. D block is where Lawrence worked and I had an uncanny feeling the presence of those vehicles must in some way be connected to him. People were standing about chatting in small groups as they brought out what appeared to be a plastic rubbish sack. Then I recognised it as a body bag. Hurrying over to the entrance, I approached the first person I recognised, Dr Fleming from the physics department. 'Gerald!' I demanded, 'What's going on? What's happened?'

'Lawrence Kennedy is dead,' he answered gravely. 'They found him hours ago. What the hell happened we have no idea!'

'Who found him?' I asked.

'Two or three people I gather. I think one of them was Janet Rowland. I saw them taking her to the sick room. Poor girl was white as a sheet.'

Janet Rowland was on temporary posting with us from the US. We'd met several times socially so she knew me quite well. I headed off to find her. At the sick room they told me she'd gone down to the canteen with some others so that's where I headed.

There were three of them including Janet, seated with cups of coffee by the window. Drawing close I observed the troubled expressions on their faces. Janet had been crying and there were crumpled tissues by her cup.

'Excuse me butting in,' I said. 'I just got back from London. I need to know what happened.'

They looked at each other, then at me, and one of the men replied, 'Dr Kennedy has been killed.'

'Yes, I saw them bringing out the -. Janet, can you tell me what happened? I was with Lawrence only a few days ago. He and I were discussing his current project.'

'Three of us found him,' she said in a hesitating half whisper. 'It - it was dreadful, Don. Really quite dreadful.'

'Better leave it, Don,' said one of the others. 'She's too upset.'

'No,' responded Janet, 'I'll be all right. I think Don ought to know. It's only fair.'

I sat down and waited whilst she drank a little more coffee.

'It was around eleven o'clock,' she began. There was an electrical storm. It was very bad - really awful and we had to shut a few things down. I was going along the ground floor corridor when I heard this - this, terrific whining – more – more a howling noise. I couldn't make out where it was coming from at first but it got even louder as I walked toward Dr Kennedy's lab. I could feel it through the floor – a sensation like a tuning fork, as if the whole building was alive. What with that and the thunder and lightning outside, I hardly knew what was going on. I saw him through the window. His room is insulated so it was no use banging on the glass.' She took a deep breath, paused for some moments then continued, 'He was staggering about, knocking stuff all over the place then clutching his head in his hands. The noise by then was terrible – a kind of continuous shrieking. I'm sure it came from inside the lab so it must have been incredibly loud in there. He - he was going crazy. He looked as if he was screaming and shouting at - I don't know - at something! It felt as though the world was crashing in on all of us. I tried his door but it was locked then I banged on the glass with my shoe.'

'He was shouting, you say. Did you see anything, anybody else in there?'

She looked at me, puzzled. 'I - I'm not sure. The lights inside the laboratory and the corridor went out at the same time. I could only see by light coming from outside the building. I thought I saw something – shadows - shadows moving around him like -.' She pressed fingers to the sides of her face and stared past me. 'No – there can't have been anyone else - just him. When the lightning flashed again I saw things breaking, instruments, furniture, all sorts of stuff flying about so I went to get help. Three of us dashed back to the lab - it can't have been more than five minutes later. The noise wasn't as bad. It was much lower like - like a dynamo running down.' She stopped and reached for a tissue. 'The lights came back on. We looked through the window and - and -.' she put a hand over her mouth and gazed down at the table in silence. One of the others touched my arm, indicating that we should move away and leave her alone. I followed him to another table and we sat down.

'Look,' he said quietly, 'the whole thing's been a dreadful shock. We overrode the door mechanism and I was one of the first inside his lab. The place was and still is a shambles. It seemed as if everything had been wrecked - equipment, fittings, the lot. Lawrence Kennedy was dead. It looked as though he'd been shaken apart - as though something - some great hand had seized him and - and -. His body was broken – smashed, crumpled like a child's toy. You'd hardly have recognised his face. There was blood everywhere. How it happened isn't - well, no one has any idea. Nobody seems to know what he was up to in there, either. He'd been working on some project all his own, apparently.'

'Yes,' I remarked, 'we were discussing it at the beginning of this week.'

'Of course - you mentioned you'd been talking to him. The police are taking statements. You'd better tell them everything you know.'

***

I related to the police and the university authorities most of what Lawrence had told me of his work but avoided mention of his more questionable conclusions. If the press had got hold of the full story who knows what the public might have been led to believe, let alone the damage it would have caused to the reputation of the university. Meanwhile, until his affairs could be sorted out, Helen and I took it upon ourselves to keep an eye on his house and to look after his cat.

Helen came with me on the evening of his death. As full of curiosity as everyone else about what had happened, she at least didn't press me with questions. Whilst she fussed over the cat, I had a look at Lawrence's recordings. There were only two on the rack - the rest must have been taken by him to the laboratory which, for the time being, was sealed off. It took me a while to figure out his system but eventually I did. Lawrence had colour coded the various playback units on the control box switches and master volume, which made it easier than it might have been to get things working.

Helen sat quietly with the cat on her lap as I inserted the disk then switched the machine to 'play.' For a time there was only silence. Then, gradually, it began. A soft, booming, swishing arose from the big speakers. It rolled about the room in a tide of sound that enveloped us totally. Helen gazed at me with apprehension, awaiting the unexpected, whilst I just stared at the player.

After a while, when we concluded that nothing spectacular was going to happen, she said, 'Why, Don - why would he go to all the trouble of recording that? It sounds like wind blowing through the trees - just meaningless sounds.'

'Yes,' I breathed, eyeing the cat, which had left her lap and now lay curled up asleep in its accustomed place, 'just wind blowing through the trees. To us, ordinary sounds. Yet those sounds meant something to Lawrence and perhaps to -.'

Helen appeared pale and anxious as she got up to slip an arm about my shoulder. 'Don, I have a nasty feeling about all this. I don't just mean over Lawrence's death. I - I mean about you getting involved in whatever he discovered. Please stay away. Tell them everything he told you.'

I understood her feelings but I'd already decided that I couldn't leave things as they were. Lawrence had stumbled upon something incredible and it had killed him. It was as if he had goaded some unseen beast into violent anger. Sooner or later we'd be allowed access to the lab and I'd get my hands on the rest of those recordings.

They must hold the key to what he'd discovered. The answer lay there and I had to know.

Memories

He had parked the car on the busy main street close to the shops because it would be less conspicuous there. Less conspicuous than if he had driven it all the way to the side street where she lived. It was an expensive car, an executive car – hired for him in advance by the corporation and collected at the airport upon his arrival in the country. Only a successful person would drive a car like that. He did not want her to see the car.

Before reaching the corner, he raised his umbrella. The suit he wore; that, too, spoke of success, or might for those who could recognise quality. If the people milling about the shops in the rain looking at the price of fruit, vegetables and meat and seeing no further than another evening of their drab lives wasted in front of the television - if they knew what this suit had cost him -. But of course, they didn't. Perhaps it was just as well. Perhaps it was as well the rain was falling and almost everyone was obscured beneath hood or umbrella. On a wet day such as this people went about their business in a diminished world, doing what they had to do, wanting only to be home again. They would take less notice of the car. Little or no notice of him. Yes, anonymity was the best thing. This was not a good area. It never had been.

The side street he now trod, the wet flagstones of the pavement reflecting the chill grey above, the cramped terraced houses with grimy brick fronts, the iron drainpipes that gushed water across his path and threatened to sully his shoes - all resurrected memories. The tapping of his heels upon the cold stone, the drumming of rain on the umbrella. All resurrected memories.

Once, he had played in those streets. Once, these rows of Victorian houses had defined the physical limits of his world. Once, long ago, he had swung about, leaned against and scratched his name with a penknife in the green paint of iron lampposts and boasted idly in dark hours under their dismal yellow light. The clatter of his feet and the feet of those he once knew had echoed about narrow, cobbled alleyways that ran behind the houses to form a secret maze through which they had stalked the nights of childhood adventure. The images returned. Rediscovered. The contents of some old cupboard that had long been wallpapered over. He recalled the small pocket torches for sending messages in the darkness. One flash - keep on to the next alley or the next street and we'll meet there. Two flashes - come this way and I'll wait. Secret messages and codes. Folded scraps of notepaper pushed between the peeling planks of back doors that hid the tiny stone flagged yards where the coal was discharged from rough sacks, where bikes were kept and Monday washing hung out if the weather was dry.

Games, intrigues, pursuits, deceptions. They were a part of the life he once knew. The measure of his childhood days. In some ways, life had changed not at all. Except now it was called high finance.

Crossing the street, he reached the corner he had turned all those years ago when passing the other way in the abandonment of his past. The little shop was still there. He hesitated to stare through

111

the window with the umbrella pushed back over his shoulder, metal drip-tips squeaking on the glass. Across an empty interior he observed the deserted counter, dimly illuminated by a single light bulb. Next to the counter, the darkened form of the games machine - an electronic mausoleum. The shop was now a Chinese take-away. Once, it had been a place of pilgrimage, a place of magic. Once it had been the paper shop. He recalled the smell of newsprint, boiled sweets, tobacco and old string. On Wednesdays, his precious comic would be put aside, waiting to spill out the images and sagas of other words and other times. Of evil tyrants and scowling beasts that fell to the righteous blows of a charging hero whose hair was never out of place. And on Saturdays, with a meagre allowance weighing lightly in his pocket, his face would press to the window, eyes eager for some new enticement that might have appeared against which to commit his pittance for the next month or more. A model gun, an aircraft or some impossible space machine. The shop had been a wonderland, a portal to other dimensions through which he might escape the drabness of that childhood world. But it was gone forever.

He turned the corner and entered the street whose flagstones he had long ago sworn never to tread again. Sworn it and meant it for his was an uncommon determination. That determination had taken him far - further than ever he had dreamt in those days of back alley skulking and in those night-times of cowering in his upstairs room above the back yard. Cowering from voices charged with anger in a house of bitterness. If they could see him now, the kids with whom he had once scurried around those drab streets. If only. A few of them might still exist here; numb behind yellowed net curtains or settled half asleep before the pointless babble of a television screen. If it wasn't for the rain, might he even now be recognised? But the street was deserted, the windows blank, some boarded up. No one would know of his return except her. He had made her promise in his letter. Made it a condition of his visit that she should tell no one.

The rain was falling harder. Falling as if it would never stop. Splashing his shoes and trousers as it gushed along the kerbside and down through the iron drains into some black hell. And there was the house, just a few steps past the next lamppost. Her house. The house he thought never to see again. Would she see him approach? Would the net curtain twitch aside to reveal her face? She would recognise him even after all these years. Surely she would. There were the photographs he had sent.

He'd not been able to give her an exact time - just early afternoon. He glanced at his gold wristwatch as he neared the door. It showed almost two forty-five though the darkening sky implied a much later hour. And here was the door, one step up and recessed under a brick arch. An anonymous, wood-panelled door that once had been painted brown. Once long ago. There was no doorbell. There never had been a doorbell. He reached up to the flaking iron knocker. It struck the iron stud three times. Not too hard in case the sound raised attention from nearby. He glanced at the houses either side. Both appeared unoccupied.

A bolt grated. A latch turned. The door opened part way and her face appeared.

He should not have been surprised. He should have expected that in the passing decades she would have changed. But his memory of her had not changed, so he was still surprised.

'Oh, you're all wet, love,' she remarked with unsmiling familiarity, as though they had spoken only hours before. 'Didn't you come in the car?'

'I walked part of the way, mother,' he replied dryly as she pulled the door wide. 'I left the car on the main road by the shops. I thought it might be easier to park.'

She was grey, stooping and small. Much smaller than he remembered. The mauve woollen cardigan hung loose about frail shoulders and the blue cotton skirt reached almost to her fur-lined slippers. As she stood back to let him enter, he glanced at her face - the face that once, long ago, had gazed down upon his. Had that gaze once held tenderness? Had it ever been caring? Perhaps. But the only face he ever recalled had been a troubled one. A face that would darken at the mention of his father. A face that had moulded to her very thoughts. A face with twitching mouth ever primed for innuendo and recrimination. Eyes and ears set to detect failings, real or imagined, in others. His father had been dead for many years, though their hapless union had dissolved long before that. From her letters he knew a kernel of hatred had endured since his father's passing and the empty husk that had been her life would not grant those memories freedom to dissipate.

'I'll put the kettle on now you're here,' she said, pushing the door shut.

From the street he had stepped directly into the small sitting room. A dim table lamp failed to liven the room. The reason, he saw, was the loose-woven green curtain draped across the lower part of the sash window – the only lighted window on the street he now concluded because there appeared to be no others. In the wall to his right, furthest from the door there was set the ornate, cast iron fireplace. On the hearth before it brightly glowed a small electric fire.

'How are you keeping?' he asked, propping his wet umbrella behind the door. About the room hung a vague odour: stale, musty, long forgotten, but rising now from the deep chasm of memory.

'Oh, I'm getting on as well as anyone at my age,' she replied. '*He* didn't leave me much as we all know. I suppose *you* live somewhere posh and fancy do you - somewhere with decent neighbours?'

'It's not bad,' he replied. 'I'm away - abroad, a lot of the time - I seldom encounter my neighbours. They're often away, too.'

'Not like these I've had to put up with I don't suppose,' she continued, lifting a discarded jumper from one of the two armchairs. 'Half of them thieves and bloody criminals if you ask me. Are you sitting down, love, or is it a flying visit after all this time?'

'It's not a flying visit,' he sighed, eyeing the few items of decrepit furniture that crouched in the shadows. 'I'm in town for the trade and finance conference on Wednesday. I flew in a day early to come and see you. I said I would in the letter.' It had always been a letter. She had no computer, of course. Not even a phone, mobile or otherwise.

She moved to the door connecting this room to the smaller one at the rear of the house that he recalled once contained a gas cooker and sink. 'Well, I hope you *are* staying more than a few minutes. I'll make a cuppa and I've got cakes and stuff. I had to go to the shops and it takes time nowadays. That's why I've not managed to tidy up yet. You'll have to excuse the place.'

'No, it's all right, he assured her, stepping to the nearest armchair and recalling that domestic pride had never been her priority. He wondered how many people could find it within themselves to be proud of a place like this. She had referred to it as a hovel when he was a child. It meant nothing then. Only after leaving did he understand. She had chosen to stay as if to prove the point, yet her journey through life could have been so much better.

As she passed into the next room he stooped over the chair to run fingers over worn fabric. A small faded cushion rested in the corner of the chair and this he picked up, brushing the fabric to dispel any dust that might lie there. Adjusting the cushion, he lowered himself with the reluctance of one entering a bath of cold water, then relaxed. In the next room a tap was running. He heard the click of the kettle lid followed by the plop of an igniting gas jet.

He mused upon the expression that had greeted him, on the familiarity of her features, still evident despite an increasing burden of years. They were a confirmation of all he remembered from childhood, a mask that did nothing to cap an oozing well of bitterness. Why? How could anyone nurture such resentment through all those years? She had not smiled when seeing him at the door because she could not smile. She had made of the house a shrine to her past and to her feelings. She could have moved elsewhere years ago. He would have paid all her bills though she was seldom short of money. He had seen to that as well, though she had never disclosed what had been done with it any more than she had rendered to him a word of thanks. It was as if she felt he owed her at least that much in recompense for his desertion. A recompense he considered it was never his to make.

Reaching into his pocket he withdrew the smart phone, checked to ensure it was switched on then placed it upon the circular wooden table close by. The phone was out of time, out of place. An intruder from a century, from a way of thinking that had never arrived here. There was no television, yet the previous year he had paid for one via the Internet and ordered it delivered to her. Perhaps it was in the next room or in her bedroom. Perhaps it was better not to ask.

He peered about the walls where hung plastic-framed prints: a cartoon cat with huge, tearful eyes, a too gaudily rendered Mediterranean village, and above the fireplace the once ubiquitous Tretchakov portrait of a green lady. He recalled them well. And there on the plain sideboard, photographs in thin, gold plastic frames. Photographs, faded and cracked, of her family; some of them dead before he was born, their frozen smiles unchanged since the day he had left the house.

She reappeared, tray in hand. 'I know you used to like your tea sweet but I've not put sugar in it. You can do your own. You used to like fruit cake so I hope this'll be all right.'

'I'm sure it will be,' he smiled.

Upon the tray rested two china cups and saucers, a bowl of sugar and a china plate bearing two slices of cake.

'I hope it's all right,' she repeated, 'I've other things in the back if not.'

'Really, it's fine,' he insisted.

You always liked fruitcake when you lived here,' she continued. 'I always had things like that in the house even when I got nothing out of him to live on. Him - the big businessman with bloody big flash car.'

'Don't you *ever* forget?' he asked, trying to conceal his irritation as he stirred the tea.

'After all I had to put up with,' she replied. 'You don't know half of what was going on. And that old reptile of a mother of his! No - you don't know the half of it!'

'Probably just as well,' he muttered, recalling the strife that once had been his daily lot. 'I'm flying to our office in Houston next week,' he offered, reopening a mental chink to the outside world. 'Houston in Texas. Oh, and I'm expecting a call from them this afternoon. It's still morning over there, you know. Yes, It'll be bright and sunny in Texas.'

'I always wanted to travel,' she commented. 'Never had the chance, I used to take you to the seaside on the coach when you were little. Used to

118

stay with your aunty Ruth. They had a nice big house.'

She arose awkwardly from the chair and moved around to the sideboard to pull open one of the top drawers. Sipping tea, he watched her lift out an ancient brown packet that appeared to have been repaired long ago with now peeling adhesive tape.

'This envelope's falling apart,' she remarked, returning to her own chair. 'I don't suppose you've been on a coach since then. I suppose you fly everywhere or get driven.'

'Mother,' he countered, 'I'm part responsible for the European end of a multinational finance corporation. I couldn't travel by coach even if I wanted to, and yes, I do sometimes have a driver because it's the way they do things.'

'That would have suited him,' she said, reaching into the envelope. 'Hand me - fetch me - carry me. Whenever he was at home sat glued to the chair or stinking in bed. Hand me, fetch me, bloody well carry me.'

'For Christ's sake,' he muttered as photographs spilled out between the cups and saucers. There he saw images from another time. Another world.

'Remember that?' she asked. The picture showed a fair-haired little boy of five or six years old, standing before a line of tall iron railings with an ice cream cone clutched in one hand.

'Not exactly,' he replied, having no recollection of when the photograph was taken, though the image itself he found disturbing in its familiarity. The next picture showed him with a small bucket and spade, digging a hole in the sand, quite oblivious of the camera. Next came a picture of the car. His father's car. Yes, he remembered that old car, an eight horse-powered car. They called it horse-power in those days, not CC's. The car was black, boxy, had chrome rimmed headlamps and chrome bumpers. It smelled inside of Bakelite, damp leather and stale tobacco. He'd forgotten the smell of that car until now. Did the car still exist? Had it survived in the hands of some dedicated collector?

In another photograph he was with her, his mother. They stood in bright sunlight by a gateway to a path that led across a rising field. She was young, slim, attractive, with flowing blond hair and wide eyes. He peered closely at her face. The picture caused him unease. It made him feel as if she still possessed a part of him and that he had never truly broken away.

'Who took this photograph?' he asked.

'Him,' she answered dryly. In that one word writhed the power of her feelings. As a child he had wanted to ask why she so detested his father but the time had never seemed right. He still wondered, still feared in case her reply might engulf, might draw him into the dark maelstrom of their past. 'Another cuppa?' she asked with perplexing indifference. 'There's more in the pot.'

Looking up from the photographs he replied, 'Oh, er, I wouldn't mind - please.'

He watched her rise, hands grasping the arms of the chair, eyes fixed unblinking as she reached for his empty cup with slightly trembling hand. She walked, almost hobbled, around obstructing old chairs to disappear from the room once again. Returning to the photographs he gazed upon monochrome images of innocence and sunlight. Most of the photographs had been taken in the countryside or by the sea. Here was one of himself sitting on a farm gate - another of him gathering pebbles on the beach. Always there was sunlight. When had this world of light ended? When had bitterness taken hold? Could the world preserved in these fading pictures ever have existed?

'Remember those cards you used to collect?' came her voice as she placed the refilled teacup in front of him.

'Cards?' he queried as she turned a second time to the drawer.

'Yes, the cards. All those cards with sportsmen. They're in here somewhere.'

As she turned, clutching the worn red album in her hands, he remembered. His cigarette cards. His collection of heroes.

'So you still have that.' he muttered, raising a hand to take the album from her. It once had him begging cards from his father and others who smoked. Most people smoked in those days. The red covered album, with parchment pages and corner slits where the cards fitted in neat rows, had come from the newsagent's shop that once had stood on the corner. The covers were begrimed and the edge of one had split to reveal the inner stiffening of grey board. Pushing aside mobile phone, plate, cup and saucer, he laid the album on the table. There in muted colours were those half-forgotten men depicted in stalwart determination - some bearded, some not. Some stood at ease, some tensed with bat poised, some clutched the hard ball, ready to spring forward. Here were men of character, men of honour and integrity. Not for them the world of instant communications, high-pressure schedules and knife-edge deals. What would they make of all that?

'They're all there,' came her voice. 'I haven't touched any of them.'

The cards appeared as neatly laid out as the day he had last gazed upon them.

'There's more.' She said. 'Lots more. I've kept everything you left. I've thrown nothing away.'

'Oh, where?' he asked.

'In the cellar,' she answered, 'Where you used to keep it all. It's still there. Everything. That model boat you used to float in rain puddles. That's there and -'

'The boat?' he cut in, 'that's still there? God, I can't have been more than ten or eleven. I thought you or the old man had chucked that out before -'

'*Him* chuck it out?' she responded. 'He'd not lift a bloody finger in this house. All he'd do was sit there and drape his coat over himself rather than get up and put a bit of coal on the fire. I had to do all that. Hand me, fetch me, bloody carry me! And if I wasn't here to do his dinner when he rolled home at all hours, he'd bugger off to the old reptile's! It was her poisoned him and the rest of them against -'

'Look!' he interrupted with barely concealed anger. 'My things. You said you'd kept all my things.'

For a moment she remained silent. Then she said casually, 'Oh, all your things are still there, yes. I can't go down any more. Not with my legs the way they are. Haven't been down in years. Her next door had an accident on the cellar stairs. She's in a care home now. Thought she was too good for everyone. Wouldn't give you the time of day.'

'I thought the houses on both sides looked rather deserted,' he remarked.

'The other side's gone off to her sister's with the two kids. Her so-called husband buggered off and left her ages ago. Men! All the bloody same.' She glanced toward the connecting door, behind which stood the entrance to the cellar. 'Bulb's gone down there. You'll need the torch.'

'I'll fix that if you've got a spare bulb,' he offered.

'I've no spare bulb,' she replied. 'Nothing like that.'

She raised herself from the chair once more and returned to the sideboard. Pulling open the drawer next to where the photographs and album had lain, she retrieved a torch, leaned over the chair and handed it to him. It was an old metal torch, once brightly chromed, now dull and dented.

'It should work all right,' she remarked, 'the man at the electrical shop put new batteries in for me last week.'

He wondered why that was if she never needed it.

He clicked the torch on and off to confirm that it worked then raised from the armchair. 'I'll take a look. Should be interesting.' But even if it was not interesting, it would help pass the time.

She watched unmoving as he strode around to the connecting door that opened to reveal the small back room and the door giving access to the cellar. Across the room stood the solid wooden door opening onto the yard and at its left, the stairs that led up to the two small bedrooms. Often had he fled up those narrow, unlit stairs to escape rage and turmoil. Well did he recall listening in darkness at the top of those stairs whilst the two who had brought him into this world spat venom at one another and raised the spectre of violence.

Set into the wall at his right stood the iron-arched fireplace, flanked by black iron ovens with heavy, steel-latched doors that as a child he imagined must lead into some primordial world. The fireplace gaped empty. His attention fell lastly upon the black canvas shopping trolley, evidently new, that stood part hidden by an old, drop-leaf table. The trolley did not belong in this time and space.

The cellar door sighed inward. Wooden steps descended, vanishing into blackness. The cellar had fascinated him as a child. He had lain awake at night as they argued downstairs, imagining himself down there, thinking that beneath seeping floor or beyond flaking walls there might exist another realm. A realm he could explore in peace and solitude - if only he possessed the secret of how to enter it. From fathomless darkness arose an odour of mouldering brick, of damp, decaying wood. A click and the torch beam stabbed downward.

The stairs descended to a floor of darkened brick. She had been wary of entering it even before his father had fitted the two stout iron bolts to the door and threatened afterwards to lock her inside. He never attempted to confine her, though she often told others that he had.

A manicured hand fell upon the bare wooden banister. Bespoke shoes touched the first step.

Noting flakes of distemper suspended in cobwebs on the wall at his side, he hesitated after a few steps to examine the sleeve of his jacket in case any had become attached to it. Down he continued until, close to the bottom of the stairs, the torch beam shifted about to illuminate stone walls and low-beamed, wooden ceiling. Hanging from a double helix of frayed wire was the light bulb, dusty and dead as an old tomb vase. One corner of the floor was sunken, its brickwork uneven and broken. Through the fractures water pooled, dark and glistening in the torchlight. The water was obviously spreading and had already encroached upon a quarter of the floor.

As his shoe touched hard brick he recalled those far off winter days when he could not venture further than the lower steps to reach his treasured possessions because of the water. There was the dead black mouth of a rusted iron fire grate and in the alcove at its right, the now rotted tea chest he once had used as a hideaway. One summer his dog had slept in there. The dog he had tried to keep in spite of her aversion and his father's indifference. A small black Scottie that, eyes bright, tail wagging, had raced along the street to greet him each day when he appeared around the corner home from school. Later his mother started to shriek at the dog, claiming it was going mad, slamming the bedroom door at night to keep it away. One day, after school, the dog was no longer there. She insisted it had disappeared from the yard into the entry that ran behind the houses and never returned. For days and nights afterwards he had searched and called its name, knowing deep down his small, ever attentive companion was gone forever.

His beam illuminated the far wall where rusted nails protruded from bare stone. Further to the right was an alcove formed against the adjacent wall by the space under the rising stairs. Within that space, hidden from view, were the shelves where still lay, so she claimed, the treasures of his childhood. Moving around the staircase, he saw them. Resting upon sheets of yellowed newspaper were the tattered remains of books, comics and small cardboard boxes, all covered by a layer of grit. In heavy silence he raised a hand to the shelf. Torchlight glinted upon a toy revolver with broken hammer. By it lay a plastic rocket ship, a lidless tin containing dull glass marbles, a comic hero's space gun that had once lit up and buzzed loudly, much to her annoyance. Its weight told him batteries still lay inside, long ago corroded and useless. Yet here was a world with hidden life, with a voice that spoke only to him.

On the shelf below rested the boat - not as big as he remembered. He had made it from odd pieces of timber, string and glue. In a box close to it lay jumbled a metal construction kit and, next to that, a battered metal cash box that must have belonged to his father. What did it contain?

Standing the torch on the upper shelf so its beam created a diffused moon on the ceiling directly above, he lifted the cash box, intending to blow dust from it. Oddly, there was little dust. He lowered the box and released the catch. Within were letters addressed in meticulous handwriting.

His letters.

He picked out and opened the first of them, sent to her only a fortnight ago, informing her of his intended visit. Beneath it lay the previous letter of three months before, posted in time for Christmas. This, too, he opened, hardly aware that the light of the torch was waning.

His letters had always been brief, almost formal in style because he had little in the way of feelings to express. Noting the dates, he realised that the letters had been placed in order of receipt so that the ones at the bottom of the cash box must be the oldest, perhaps the very earliest he had sent to her. Could it be she had kept even those? He lifted out most of the letters and placed them aside on the shelf. The light from the torch was without a doubt weakening. He became aware of closing shadows.

The few remaining letters were indeed the first. Here was the letter he had written within a year of fleeing this house of despair to find a world of freedom from which he could look back and express his true thoughts. And he had done exactly that. Taking the letter from the bottom of the box, he opened and read those first words. In the undisciplined hand of earlier years was penned his rejection of her, his father, and the life he had endured with them. Rejection of her and of a father who had not long before taken himself off, leaving them to fend for themselves. He was surprised by the vehemence and condemnation of his earlier words. What must have been her reaction as she read them? She had never referred to that first letter.

The torch flickered as he separated the second and third letters then he stopped to peer closer. Something quite familiar lay between. He withdrew the postcard and held it close to the torch. On one side was a photograph of the company offices in Houston. On the other, only a date and his signature. The card had been included with the letter he had sent to her before leaving America. It was only three weeks old and stated his intention to undertake this visit. It must have fallen from the top envelope to become lodged between those at the bottom when they were removed from the cash box. She must have read through those earlier letters. Perhaps days, perhaps only hours, before his arrival. Perhaps standing in this very spot.

Only minutes before, she had claimed she had been unable to enter the cellar in years.

The light from the torch had become a feeble, pallid yellow. The batteries cannot have been new. In encroaching darkness he heard the floorboards creak above. He had not heard the cellar door close, had not heard the two iron bolts slip across. Already she had put on her raincoat, purple woollen scarf and plastic rain hood then, grasping the handle of the shopping trolley that contained her few valuables, some items of clothing and the photographs of her family, she stepped through into the front room, turning only to close the connecting door. There she reached to collect his mobile phone from the coffee table, then the still wet umbrella from where he had placed it. A muffled shout reached her ears as she twisted the latch to open the front door. Then a dull hammering. She glanced at the terraced houses opposite. That side of the street had been ready for the demolition men weeks ago. Later this afternoon, on her side, they would switch off the electricity and gas. She was last to leave the street.

She found it no easy task in manoeuvring the loaded trolley down the step. Again the shouting - more distant now. Gripping the doorframe to steady herself, she looked back into the house, muttering, 'Just like his bloody father. Never gave a bugger about anyone as long as he had what he wanted. Never around when he was needed. Just cleared off.'

Rain beat against the flagstones as she slammed the door. Gazing along the deserted street she pulled the hood tighter and recalled what the man on the radio had said. It would rain heavily like this for the next few days, then it would turn colder. Well, what did they expect this time of the year? The cellar would soon be two or three feet deep in black water. And when the demolition men moved in the houses would be reduced to rubble under a cloud of billowing dust. Bricks, mortar, roof slates, windows - all would succumb to machines shrieking louder by far than a human cry.

The path leading down to the canal was difficult for one whose legs were not strong. The trolley dragged, so from time to time she halted to steady herself by rusted iron railings. Once at the canal progress was easier, though the towpath was narrow. People walked along here when the weather was fine. Under ragged sky, in chill rain, it was quite empty.

The canal passed close by the bus station. It would be difficult dragging the trolley back up to the main road but there was plenty of time. It was at least an hour before the coach left for the seaside town where her sister lived in the new home funded by her compensation and *his* money.

A warbling sound caused her to stop. Leaning over the trolley, she unzipped the flap, reached inside, lifted out the mobile phone. Taking care not to approach too close to the edge of the towpath, she cast the alien object over the side then watched as, still demanding a response, it vanished beneath sluggish grey, rain-pitted water. The umbrella drifted some way from the embankment before it, too, sank from sight.

The wheel had turned full circle. At long last she could forget.

Dollshouse

The burning outback spread forever wide, exposed and dry-boned. An arid vastness under the blue dome of an empty sky. A moving speck passed insect-like across this elemental sweep, raising a plume of fine red dust that drifted to oblivion in the warm air.

Soon after sunrise they left the highway but driving was not so troublesome. Not if they kept a wary eye for the occasional, obtrusive rock. A lizard scampered from their path, its microcosm of burning sand, spinifex and twisted mulga violated in the brief moment of their passing. Some time after midday, when the heat bore down at its most intense, the camper van drew to a halt by a stand of gnarled acacia. Here they rested for a while, the growl of their engine yielding to the bluster of desert air that forever carried a tang of eucalyptus and scorched wood.

'How's this compare with city life?' he smiled, opening his shirt to the waist as they sat on the ground in the narrow shade of the van.

'Real nice,' she smiled back, 'I've never been right out in the sticks before. Never so far away from the coast. Never so far from other people.'

'Feels like we own the place, doesn't it? All of it - ours.'

She rested her head against the van, feeling the heat of metal on her scalp and smelling warm engine oil. She reached to the lid of the cool-box. 'Maybe, Kevin. Maybe it's the other way about - maybe it owns us. Out here feels big enough to own everything.'

'Jeez, no Kerry - nothing owns us.' He took the chilled beer she offered, snapped open the can, drank gratefully. 'We go where we please - over the desert, on to the next town, stop when and where we want. We up and go whenever the mood takes us. We're free, Kerry, you and me. Free as the birds.'

They ate, drank, talked and laughed until the stillness of the desert submerged their thoughts and shadows turned around the acacias.

'It's too hot now,' she said at last. 'Too hot even here in the shade.'

Easing himself up, he pulled the brim of his bush hat down then dropped empty cans into the white plastic bag. She stood by him, one hand shading her eyes, the other holding straw blond hair against her cheek. Waiting.

'If you like,' he said, 'I'll call up Woodruff's Creek. There's a half-decent little hotel there. It's hardly Adelaide but I reckon we could make it before ten or eleven if we turn west a bit and join the highway. The road can't be very far. Not now.'

She zigzagged a finger down his chest and smiled, 'No, Kev, we can do without other people's company for a while longer. Besides, everything we need is in the van. You said so.'

'OK by me, but I reckon you'll be missing civilisation before we reach Palmersville. You see if I'm right.'

'What you mean is you'll be getting low on grog. That's what you really mean.'

'Mind reader,' he grinned, and swung open the van door. 'Better get on board, the bus service around here is pretty crook!'

The engine growled to life as she settled in beside him, grateful for overworked air conditioning that would soon bring down the temperature. 'Kev, when we stop at a place like this I feel - I feel sad about going. I feel I want to leave something, a token, a coin maybe, just to show someone once lingered for a while. Just so it remembers us. That would make it special forever. Don't you think?'

'Yeah, I know, it feels like that out here sometimes. Like nobody ever came that way before and nobody ever will again.'

The camper van moved on with memories of laughter and a small stand of acacias lost beneath a fathomless sky. Already the warm breeze had softened their tracks and footprints. Soon, all trace of their passing would be gone.

***

They were heading due north and by late afternoon a range of low hills, hazed greyish-mauve in a lowering sun, appeared across the horizon to their right.

'Kev, can you make out what that is?'

'What? Where am I looking?'

'There - over to the right. Looks like a small farm.'

'A farm? Yeah, I see it. Who'd set up a farm out here in the middle of nowhere?'

'Well, it's something Kevin. Farm or no, let's take a look.'

'Aw, no one'll live there now. What's the point?'

'Point is, we have to stop sooner or later to cook supper and rest up. It'll make a change from the van if there's anywhere to sleep and maybe it'll be cooler.'

'OK, Kerry, we'll give her a try if you'll do some driving tomorrow.'

'Sure, Kev, I'll drive tomorrow.'

***

The house stood stark white against desert and dark hills, picked out by a low sun that flamed twists of cloud against a deepening sky.

'Abandoned decades ago, I reckon,' he commented as they drew closer and began to slow. 'Probably full of -'

'Kevin! Look - oh!'

He followed her gaze toward an upper window as the camper van shuddered to a halt. 'Well?'

Nose against the windscreen, she kept her eyes fixed for seconds more. 'I thought I saw a face. Someone up there was watching us. Looking right at us. Just for a moment.'

'OK, if there is someone, they'll come down and we'll see them for sure.'

'Give it a minute Kev - a minute before we get out.'

'Half a minute! We've been here thirty seconds already.'

They remained silent for a while then he grinned, 'I told you, not even the dingoes live around here. C'mon, let's get out.'

They stood together in front of the house, their shadows spilling along the ground to reach a little way up parched and flaking timber. It was cooler now and the scent of eucalyptus lay heavy on the air. He thrust hands into his pockets and cocked his head. 'Can you hear something - a tapping sound?'

'It's around the side I think,' she replied. 'Yeah, it's around there.'

'Tell you what Kerry, I'll take a stroll and see while you get out the beers and the grub. If I don't come back, you can have my share!'

'Forget it sport!' she responded, digging him in the ribs. 'I'm coming along, too. And we both know whose turn it is to do the cooking.'

As they walked, she said, 'D'you know what this place reminds me of?'

'I guess not,' he answered. 'What does it remind you of?'

'It's like one of those surrealist paintings. You know - Salvador Dali. All white, standing on the red earth with those purple hills behind. And the sky - and look - look at that ghost gum! Did you ever see anything so weird? Nearly all the branches are gone.'

'Weird, that's for sure. Looks like the finger of a skeleton pointing up into the sky. He'd have to be a giant though, wouldn't he?'

'Oh, and look at these timbers, Kev.'

They stooped to run fingers over tortured wood. Saw grain split apart in desiccated agony with eye-socket knotholes staring blindly from the wooden boards. 'Dry,' he breathed, 'Dry as old bones.'

'Yes, the corpses of once living trees.'

They moved in silence about the house, passing into long shadows at the rear.

'Hey, Kerry there's a well inside that enclosure. Maybe it still has water.'

'Is that where the noise was coming from?'

'Dunno - let's take a look.'

A black emptiness filled their gaze as they peered over the low wall. Under the contorted wooden beam, a shred of dry rope still swung above the centre of the stone circle, tapping against one of the wooden supports.

'Nothing,' he said, 'too dark to see but I reckon it'll be dry.'

A short distance from the well lay a metal skeleton hung with corroded plates. At one end of it, bared and exposed, emerged a small hulk of rusted machinery.

'Jeez!' he exclaimed, 'will you take a look at this old car! The sand's almost over her wheels.'

Kerry put a hand on his shoulder. 'Oh, you'd hardly tell it was a car at all would you. How long d'you think she's been here?'

'Hard to say,' he pondered. 'She's got be 1930's - maybe older. Must have been a beaut car in her day. Wonder why she was left to rot away like this.' Circling about, he tried to imagine the proud, polished lines this forsaken relic once possessed. The car reassembled in his mind - a living machine, a gleaming, graceful object of pride and purpose. He pondered upon what use it could have been to the people who once occupied the house

'Hey Kevin! Come and take a look at this!' Her voice drifted from what had been the hidden side of the house. The car dissolved back into ruin.

He stepped around the corner to find her staring at the ground. 'It's a grave, Kev. Someone's been buried here.'

On the earth by the side of the house was laid out a rectangle of small stones. Each picked out in the orange glow of the lowering sun, each casting a dark finger of shadow. Tilted at an angle, the small headstone might have been about to fall but was still held firmly in the earth. The girl bent down in front of it, running fingers over incised letters. In the slanting light, the name was not difficult to read. 'Emily – that's all it says, no date, no age. Just Emily. I wonder who she was.'

'Just a kid from the size of the grave, I reckon.'

'It feels so sad here Kevin - so very sad.' Her fingers remained resting on the headstone, her thoughts deep as the well. Kevin watched in silence then after a time, took her hand. They walked on until once again they stood at the front of the house where the camper van waited. On the horizon, a red sun merged into glowing haze whilst clouds billowed towers of flame and shadow. The breeze was gone, the stillness solemn and intense, its silence broken only by the electric murmur of cicadas.

'Maybe we should take a peek inside before it gets dark,' he said, stepping to the door. 'You grab the torch.'

The door, a geometric mockery of what it once was, opened on protesting hinges. Their shadows merged into obscurity, framed by the dying glow to the west. Across the room, as their eyes adjusted to the darkness, could be seen another door, partly ajar and leading into what the girl fancied must be a small kitchen. 'Kev,' she whispered, 'there are still a few old bits of furniture and - hey, look at those pictures on the wall.'

Wooden floorboards creaked softly as they moved inside the room to stand side by side, eyes fixed upon the pictures.

'It's the same little girl in all of them,' she whispered as the light of their torch flickered from one to the other. 'I reckon it's little Emily.'

'Could be,' he answered, gazing about, 'but I don't reckon there'll be anything of any use here. Not after all this time.' They moved about, tugging drawers open to find only yellowed sheets of newspaper without any dates, then pulling open small cupboard doors that squeaked on age-afflicted hinges. 'The pictures, Kerry, I wonder why they didn't take them when they went away.'

'Maybe they wanted to leave their memories behind. Maybe they wanted to gather everything about her life here, even the photographs. Maybe they wanted nothing of Emily to leave the house.'

Peering into the small, dim kitchen Kerry observed broken wooden tub, warped and empty shelves hazed by spider webs, and a flaking enamel basin abandoned in one corner. Handing him the torch, she trod warily to the small staircase.

Suddenly, a scream, and he turned wide-eyed. 'What the -!'

'Jesus, Kevin it's a bloody snake!'

Kerry stood clutching her cheek with one hand, her other gesturing to the foot of the stairs as he peered into the shadows. Gleaming in the light of his torch, the creature's black and pale-banded form writhed and uncoiled. It arched its back then disappeared from sight through a gap in the planking.

'She's pretty harmless,' he laughed. 'Just a Bandy-Bandy - more scared of you than you are of her, I reckon.'

138

'No it bloody well isn't, Kevin! I'm definitely more scared of it than it is of me! Struth! I nearly had a heart attack!'

'Well don't have one just yet, sweetheart. Let's take a look upstairs.'

Placing a toe on the lowest step to test his weight, he stepped up to a second and a third. 'Should be OK. Feels solid enough. You coming?'

'Sure I am - and if we see another bloody snake I'll try not to scream until you've positively identified it!'

Kerry followed him upward into grey silence, their feet imprinting a fine dust that covered sighing timbers. The stairs entered directly into a small bedroom, illuminated only by the afterglow of a now vanished sun.

'Look at those wooden bunks,' she breathed, regarding the only items of furniture in the room. She felt now she ought not to raise her voice but did not consider why.

'Yeah, just bare planks,' he answered. 'I reckon our blankets would do the job nicely on those. What d'you say - do we give it a go?'

'I might, Kevin, if you check underneath first.'

Looking aside, Kerry observed a door. It corresponded to the position of the kitchen entrance on the floor below. Kevin peered about the diminutive bedroom, kneeling low to shine his light into the darkness beneath the two bunks. 'Nothing to be scared of down here,' came his voice. 'No spiders, no snakes - nothing.'

'I just have to see inside there,' she whispered, pushing by him. She twisted the iron handle. The door squeaked ajar at her touch and she eased cautiously inside. The air hung still. Timeless as a long forgotten shrine. Within the room vague forms emerged from silent obscurity. Kerry stood, lips parted, and as he joined her she breathed, 'Oh, Kev, look - this little room is full of her things.'

Slipping an arm about her waist, he peered over her shoulder. At one side of the room under the small, dust-streaked window with darkening sky beyond, rested a child's cot - once painted bright, now sad and peeling. Against the opposite wall, waiting for its small rider through endless days and nights, stood a crude wooden rocking horse with peg-eyes and shredded-rag hair on a broomstick neck. Above the rocking horse, in a gilt oval frame, his torch picked out a sepia photograph. From it stared the face of a little girl, light hair falling about her shoulders, pale eyes gazing out from a vanished world. In deeper shadow at the far end stood a table upon which rested a large doll's house. Kerry moved into an all but tangible silence.

'Oh, it's so beautiful, so lifelike,' she breathed, stepping closer. Transfixed by what stood before her, she stooped to gaze at quaint little chimneys, at the delicately painted façade and the tiny upstairs windows with minutely leaded panes of glass.

'Kerry!' his voice rang through the heavy air. 'I'm off to get the barbecue started. It's getting pretty dark in here - d'you want the torch?'

'No – it's all right. I'll be down there in a minute. And, Kev - please don't shout.'

She waited until his footsteps had retreated down the stairs and through the room below. Now alone, breathing very softly, aware of her own heartbeat, she peered through the tiny windows of

140

the doll's house. Peered through attic rooms under a steep-pitched roof, into bigger rooms on the floor below. On the ground floor there were intricately furnished reception and drawing rooms where diminutive, colourful pictures adorned the walls. Ornate lamps stood on finely carved, miniature cupboards and tables. Everything was set about in exquisite detail. Panelled doors held minute brass knobs. Elegant wall coverings, rugs and carpets in detailed pattern graced the interior. Fireplaces held decorative brackets that supported mantle shelves upon which stood bright, impossible clocks keeping microcosmic time.

She looked aside. The room about her was almost dark and yet –. 'I can see it all so clearly,' she whispered, peering back into the house. 'Yes, all so clearly. There's light from somewhere. Oh, it's from those tiny lamps, yes, like all the people are there just waiting to step into these pretty little rooms from the back of the house. Maybe they're waiting for her to come back and play. This must have been the centre of little Emily's world, her pride and joy, everything she knew and loved. Perhaps a part of her still lives within it.'

Outside, the van door slammed. Kerry raised her head, blinked in a warm intimacy that begged her not to go. 'Jeez! What's getting into me?'

Light from the camping lantern shone through the front door as she trod downward, her hand clutching the loose wooden rail, her gaze fixed upon the bottom of the stairs in case the snake had returned. Was it a child's laughter she imagined when a silver trinket of sound tumbled through obscurity from the room above?

***

Perched on the fold-out seat, Kerry watched him shuffle steaks around in the pan, listened to them sizzle and spit over the flames, breathed in the worldly odour of cooking meat. 'Why would anybody want to set up home out here? How could they hope to make a living?'

'Dunno,' he answered. 'Maybe things were different then. Might have been wetter. A few rainy seasons, streams flowing. It would have looked greener and there'd be no other settlers around long enough to remember otherwise. Or maybe there were other people nearby.'

'A mining town?' she suggested.

'Could be in these parts. Maybe it's between here and the hills – or what's left of it.'

'I wonder who they were and what happened to them.'

'Most likely Pommies - and we know what happened to one of them.'

'Yes, Kev. She must have played out here with her toys and her little rocking horse. This house, this bit of desert - it would be all she knew. She must have been so very lonely.'

'She probably had brothers and sisters. People had big families in those days.'

'No, Kev. She's the only child in those photographs. There were no others.'

'Could be they settled out here for that reason, Kerry, to be alone, to get away from other people.'

'Give me the town anytime,' she sighed, 'even though it's good to be away from all the noise and traffic once in a while.'

'Those photographs,' he said, cutting into the steak, 'the way people in them were dressed - they must be a century or more old. Old photographs like that, in those frames - they could be worth a few dollars to an antique dealer. Maybe they'd sell on the internet. And that doll's house you were looking at, we could make room in the camper van and -.'

'Kevin, no! We mustn't! We mustn't take away those things! They're hers!'

'Struth, Kerry, there's no one left here now! The old place will fall down eventually - then what will any of it be worth?'

'Well it isn't going to fall down yet. Maybe not for years, and nobody else has been and taken anything.'

'Somebody came here. What about that old car? Nobody would need a car like that out here.'

'Beats me, Kev,' she replied, lifting a can of beer from the cool-box. Whoever it was didn't see fit to steal anything. They didn't even take away the car.'

'Yeah, maybe you're right and we leave it all alone to the desert. What's it worth in the end?'

'Yes, Kev, what is it worth?'

They had eaten and talked, and a half moon hung low in the sky when he said, 'Look, it's a beaut night with all the stars so clear. D'you want to sleep outside rather than in the van or in that old house? We'll need to get away by sunrise tomorrow.'

'Not out here, thanks,' she answered. 'Not with that Bandy - what d'you call it, skulking around.'

'The Bandy-Bandy? I told you, she's harmless unless you're a small lizard!'

'All right, Kev, that one may be but there could be others that aren't harmless. And you know how I attract insects, especially the mossies. I'm flavour of the month all year round so being the pampered city girl I am, I'd rather sleep indoors. Upstairs in that old house would be fine by me.'

'And fine by me Kerry. Tomorrow will be a great day. We'll get up early while the air is cool and fresh.'

***

On the threshold of the house, a small lizard started in the night, head twitching in tiny spasms. Now rock-still it listened, bright-eyed, waiting. Suddenly it moved - darted from the step and vanished into realms of darkness, frightened by the rodent-squeak of iron hinges as the front door closed.

Soon, Kevin and Kerry were asleep.

***

'Hello!'

'Hi – you're Emily aren't you?'

'Yes, are you my new friends?' Her face was round and happy. Her eyes playtime bright.

'Sure we are, Emily - your best friends.'

'What's your name?'

'I'm Kerry and this is Kevin. Uncle Kevin if you like.'

'I want to go out and play. Will you come and play with me? I want to play hide and seek.'

'Yes. Shall we hide from Uncle Kevin? Shall we let him try to find us?'

'Yes! Let's hide – let's hide – let's hide!'

'Jeez, listen to her laugh! You made her laugh Kerry. You're good with kids.'

144

'And after dark, will you and Uncle Kevin read me a story? I've got lots of lovely books.'

'Yes, we'll read to you tonight. We'll read to you every night.'

'Yes, Emily, we'll read every night and play every day.'

'Let's go now. Let uncle Kevin hide his eyes and count and count and count! There are lots of places to hide. Places that go on for ever and ever and ever!'

***

Their warm cocoon of sleep dissolved as the first light of morning filtered into the room.

'Kerry, are you awake?'

'Yes – I'm awake. I – I've been dreaming. Such a long dream. So real.'

'Dreaming - yes, I've been dreaming too. A long dream.'

'What did you dream, Kev?'

'About the little girl. About Emily, and you.'

'Same for me. I thought it would never end. We were like kids again, too. You and me.'

'Kerry, did we dream the same dream?'

'Maybe. We were with her - playing in the sun, dancing under the stars, laughing through the seasons, running, turning through the ages.'

'Kerry, two people can't dream the same like that. It isn't possible.'

'I don't know, Kev. It felt like a world without time. A world where the clocks all stop, then start up again without any reason,'

'Maybe one of us was talking in our sleep and the other heard. I reckon that's how it happened.'

'Kevin I feel cold. Why is it so cold?'

'Because it's early. It's just getting light. I'm cold, too.'

'Kev, what are we going to do?'

'Do? What d'you mean?'

'I mean, here. How are we going to deal with this?'

'Deal with it? Struth! This is bloody weird!' He threw aside the blanket and swung from the bunk, steadying himself with a look of surprise when he found his legs weak and aching. 'We pull ourselves together, Kerry, that's how we deal with it and we get started pretty bloody quick!'

Kerry rose unsteadily and kissed him. 'Yes, Kev, you're right - we have to leave soon.'

She began to fold the blankets then hesitated. 'Were these blankets ours? I can't remember.'

'Can't have been ours,' he muttered. 'They're too old.'

'D'you want some breakfast, Kev? Just coffee, maybe?' She laid the blankets aside, stepped across the room, paused by the door and turned to him. 'Well?'

'No,' he replied. 'Let's give it a miss. I don't feel like anything.'

'Me neither,' she shrugged and disappeared down the stairs, her footsteps confident in the lightening dawn. Kevin gazed at cracked and peeling walls, at the closed door leading into the private world where Emily's portrait hung; where stood the rocking horse and the doll's house. He took a deep breath, strode across the room and reached to open the door. His fingers had barely touched the handle when he heard her scream. In moments, he was careering down the stairs to where she stood framed in the doorway with her back to him, hands pressed to the sides of her face. Kerry turned. She stared at him in wide-eyed horror. 'Kevin - the van. Look at the bloody van!'

Pushing by her he hesitated in the doorway, hands clutching the wooden frame. Long seconds passed before the words came. 'Jesus - it can't be! It's a - it's a bloody wreck!'

Where the camper van had stood there lay a corroded hulk, part filled with red sand. Metal ribs clawed at the blue sky, strands of dry grass swayed from amidst them in the morning breeze.

'This can't be true Kerry – we're dreaming still. Tell me we're dreaming!'

'No, Kev,' she sobbed, stepping out to join him, 'we're not dreaming. Not anymore. The dream is ended.' She turned, re-entered the house, crossed the room and walked slowly up the stairs. For a while Kevin peered into the desert. Then he followed after her.

Each faced the other, seated on the bunks in which they had slept.

'It's like that old car out the back,' he said, gazing by her to the bedroom door. 'Eaten away, rotted, as though it's been there for ages.'

She remained silent, staring down at her hands where they rested in her lap.

'You know how far it is to Woodruff's Creek?' he continued. 'We've no food, we've no water and my bloody mobile phone's a lump of dead plastic. We've no chance out there in the heat, Kerry. No chance at all!'

'No,' she whispered. 'No chance at all.'

He stood up, paced the room several times then stopped by the window. The house cast a long shadow in the rising sun. Beyond stretched the desert. It had changed. Not in any way he understood. Not in any way he could explain. But it had changed.

From behind came her voice. 'She wanted friends, Kev, people to talk to, someone to share her world. It's so lonely here. So very lonely.'

'This is crazy!' he yelled. 'We're getting out of here! We're going now!'

'Where to, Kev? Where are we going?'

'I dunno! We'll walk. We'll go toward the hills. We'll just keep on walking until we reach somewhere!' Striding to the window, he stared out across the desert. Something moved in the distance. 'Hey, Kerry! Come and look! There's someone out there - someone heading this way!'

'Where?' she asked, peering over his shoulder.

'There, see! They're coming our way. Jeez, did you ever see a car like that? Come on, let's get down there quick in case they go on by!'

She hurried to the stairs and he followed. At the top she staggered as if losing her balance. Reaching out to catch her by the arm, his hand passed through a fading image. They were falling together - swirling, drifting in silence, descending slowly as a vortex of pale dust.

***

The vehicle stopped. Three young men peered up at the house.

'It's the light playing tricks,' said one, 'The place is derelict.'

'Well,' said the driver,' I'll swear someone was watching us from that upstairs window as we approached.'

'I'll take a look inside,' offered the second man. 'I could do with stretching my legs.'

'Sure thing,' agreed the third. 'I'll open some beers now we're stopped.'

The man got out and approached the house, skirted the rotted metal hulk then hesitated on seeing the nest of lizards in the frayed remains of the driver's seat. His companions watched him push through the front door. Moments later he emerged, looking over his shoulder as he hurried back.

'D'you find anything?' asked one.

'Did I!' exclaimed the man. 'It bloody nearly found me - biggest bloody snake I ever saw!'

'What colour?'

'Brown, yeah, and well over two metres long. Bloody Taipan if you ask me!'

'More likely a Mulga snake,' offered the third man, lifting the can to his lips.

'Yeah,' laughed the driver, 'you could be right. Go and take a closer look. See if it has a label on it. We'll wait!'

'No, let's drink up and get moving. There's nothing here. Nothing at all.'

***

The house brooded in a desert of vastness. Within, a sigh of wind through dried timbers. In the half-light, in the sanctuary stillness of an upstairs room, the rocking horse creaked back and forth. In the doll's house, minute lamps glowed crystal bright in miniature rooms. Tiny clocks with busy pendulums ticked away the seasons and the years, chiming as bright pins the endless hours. The sound of a child echoed, running, laughing, appearing, disappearing, playing hide and seek with her memories through spectral facets of time.

Obsession

The last thing I wanted was another crisis after all I'd been through and this was the first chance I'd had in months for the break I sorely needed. I'd still be working, yes – but working on my own terms on freelance magazine features I had planned months before rather than the superficial, over-inflated newspaper articles that were always wanted yesterday. Then there had been my divorce – a messy affair even though there was no third party involved. By now I was feeling pretty threadbare. I needed something and someone new in my life but for the time being I'd hide away.

In mid-November I was renting a small but tastefully converted eighteenth century farmhouse only a ten-minute walk from Lychbury high street. The house stood back from the main road and was concealed by trees. It possessed an atmosphere that suited my mood. It and the surrounding countryside freed my mind. Bare trees and winter landscapes hold for me a brooding fascination.

Lychbury was an old Cheshire village with a modern estate, occupied mainly by well-heeled people. It spread away from one side of the village centre and, thankfully, was not visible from the main street. Half way along this nestled the Admiral Hawke, a seventeenth century pub where, bottle of Cabernet Sauvignon close to hand, I'd often be seen perched in an alcove, oblivious to the other customers, mobile phone switched off as it almost always was, fingers scampering over the keys of my laptop.

A short distance along the opposite side of the high street stood the medieval church with, close by it, a small Norman chapel. I'd already checked over both to figure out what was original and what was Victorian restoration. It's one of those interests that looped me out of a too pressured, over-complicated world and reminded me of how people once lived a very different kind of life. I harboured no illusions, however, about their lifestyle being any better.

Foggy days were not uncommon round that time of the year so on one such afternoon, after I'd been there a couple of weeks, when the lights and life of the village were smothered by a cold grey shroud, I took to exploring the graveyard. Now I'm not prone to stalking graveyards but this one possessed an intense atmosphere of its own, especially when mists lay across the land. The place also held a bone-chilling, penetrating damp that defied almost anything you'd normally be wearing so, with my breath hanging on the air, I lit a cigarette by way of consolation. It would soon be getting dark; in fact it had never really been light that day so I wasn't surprised to find there was no one else about.

Having finished the cigarette I was of a mind to take myself back along the road to somewhere more warm and worldly when I noticed a splash of bright colour against monochrome gloom. They were flowers. Sure, I know - flowers are what you expect to find in a graveyard - but not in that particular part of that particular graveyard. It was old. Not just old but ancient. I tugged my coat tighter to preserve a warmth that was determined to find every possible escape route, then pushing hands deep into my pockets I stepped over for a closer look. The gravestones were wet and mouldering, some of them tilted, a few of them broken. The one in question, the one that had attracted my attention, stood close to a tree. When in full leaf the tree would have obscured it but now only water drops clung to skeletal twigs and bare branches. The flowers at the base of the headstone appeared to be fresh so I figured someone had placed or misplaced them there and that maybe, to look so fresh, they were plastic. I bent down to touch. The flowers were real and had been planted directly into the soil as if they were actually growing there. Being so close to the gravestone I tried to read the inscription - a task made none too easy in dim light when much of the detail appeared to have been exfoliated. I could pick out a name, Jane Lockhart, and her year of birth, 1742. The rest was unreadable except for the odd character.

Maybe it wouldn't have meant anything to most people, but it did to me. Why would anyone leave flowers on a three hundred-odd year old grave when others all about had been long abandoned to the rasping tongue of time? The sky was darkening but I stood looking at the grave until numbing cold flagged up a more sensible alternative.

Later that evening, in the Admiral Hawke, I waived the habit of keeping myself more or less to myself and enquired about Jane Lockhart and the grave. What was her situation in Lychbury and who at the present time might place flowers before such an old and decaying gravestone?

Neither the publican nor any member of his bar staff had any idea who she was. A girl standing at the bar asked, 'What kind of flowers were they on her grave?'

Never too well informed on the identity of flowers I answered, 'Red carnations – I think.' Then I proceeded to describe them.

'Yes,' the girl smiled, 'that sounds like red carnations. How romantic.'

'Perhaps her descendants still live around here,' the publican added. 'A few families have been in the Lychbury area for generations - back to Tudor times in some cases.'

'That could be,' suggested a man sitting close by. 'Or some of her family or her successors might have cleared off to America or Australia and a descendent came back over here to look up their ancestors.'

'Ay, that'll be it,' agreed the publican. 'It'll be a memento to someone's ancestor. Why not check out the parish records? See if anyone got there before you on this one.'

'An interesting idea,' I responded, but I had one of my own. There was a flower shop in the village so I would go and ask who'd recently bought red carnations. Simple.

The following day was brighter and breezier with the mists cleared away, though every bit as cold. The woman and her teenage assistant in the small flower shop were certain that no one had asked for red carnations over the last week or so. Then apart from a visit to the village delicatessen and bakery at lunchtime for a bite to eat I remained at the house, working until desire for something more than a ham sandwich determined my course of action.

It was after dark when I left the house equipped with my torch as the path to the road was unlit. There was another reason for the torch on that particular night. I intended to revisit the grave of Jane Lockhart before crossing back to the Admiral Hawke. Strolling along, pausing only to light a cigarette, I again asked myself why I should be so fascinated by something that probably was of no importance at all. But I was – and compellingly so.

Entering the churchyard through a small gate on the main street I switched the torch back on and headed for the grave in the hope that no one passing by would report the suspicious figure lurking there in the dead of night. The flowers were still there and, picked out in my torchlight, looked as fresh as on that previous afternoon. I had an idea. If I bent close to the gravestone and shone my torch from the edge, it might pick out details that were too elusive when viewed the way they had been on my first visit. I crouched low. There was water dripping down on me from the branches of the tree. Some of the drops fell into my hair, tickling my scalp then running down my neck with a touch of icy fingers. The light of my torch picked out plenty of detail on the slab, but it wasn't the sort I'd hoped for. As well as flaking stonework I found myself staring at blotches of pallid lichen. No more of the wording in the stone could be read than I had previously resolved. It had simply crumbled away.

I was about to straighten up when someone spoke my name.

It breathed softly about my ears – 'Jonathan.' Then again – 'Jonathan.'

We've all heard the old cliché, "It's only the wind in the trees," and that's what it had to be because the branches were swishing gently to and fro close above. Yet with an inexplicable intimacy the night seemed to close about as I squatted there. The world beyond no longer mattered. I rested my hand on cold stone and for a time I didn't want to move. Then as if someone had shaken me by the shoulder, I stood up with my torch beam full on the gravestone. I was shivering with cold. In my mind the lights of the Admiral Hawke shone as a beacon of salvation.

The barman smiled and offered small talk amidst general chatter as I waited for my food. 'At least we can see where we're going out there,' he said.

'Ruddy fog's coming back in a day or so,' put in an elderly man seated nearby. I lifted my first glass of wine and thought again about those carnations.

The Admiral Hawke was closing as I walked home through darkness trailing cigarette smoke, trying to conjure up an image of Jane Lockhart. The image grew in my mind as if I'd already seen a picture of her. It vied for my attention when later I sat watching television. By the time I'd trudged up to bed I was convinced I knew exactly what she once looked like. I lay there thinking she was young, fair and possessed bright eyes of vivid blue. She was very beautiful. But, of course, she had to be.

***

I was wandering down a sunlit street on a summer day when I spotted her on the opposite side. I didn't know where I was or why – nor did I care. There were people going to and fro, talking and laughing, quite oblivious to my presence. Only the girl was real. She was walking away from me, sometimes visible, sometimes not. I hurried to catch up with her, dashing across the road, pushing by those vague people then shouting, 'Hello - wait!'

She stopped and turned, flaxen hair swaying loose about her shoulders. As I drew close she smiled, 'Jonathan.' She wore a plain white cotton dress, low cut at the front but not too short. I could see no earrings, no adornments of any kind.

'Where are you going?' I asked, stepping up to her.

'Oh, I'm out walking. It's such a beautiful morning. And you, Jonathan – where are you going today? Will you walk with me?'

As I stood there sunlight glinted in her eyes. 'I – I'm just out and about,' I replied. 'Nothing important.' I had yet to speak her name.

'Will you walk with me?' she asked again.

'Sure, but -.'

'We can walk along to the churchyard. We can sit there and you can tell me all about yourself. It's such a lovely day.'

Only now, as I stood looking about did I realise I was in Lychbury. The trees were green, the sky an unreal blue and the air smelled sweet. I had no desire to go anywhere other than where she wanted.

'OK, Jane,' I said and we started to cross the road. We'd not quite reached the other side when I heard music playing. It felt like someone had poured cold water over me. She stared hard into my eyes as if I'd hurt her feelings.

***

I looked about the bedroom, dazed and confused. The radio had switched on and the readout displayed seven-thirty. I struggled upright in bed with fingers pressed over my eyes, muttering, 'What the hell's going on?' I could hear her voice receding and the wavering image of a face, her face, hovered for some moments longer. I tumbled out of bed and lurched across to the bathroom in semi-darkness, wishing I'd never set the radio alarm.

After a shower and cup of strong coffee I logged on to the parish records office in the hope of gleaning whatever information they might hold about Jane Lockhart. The records of that period for Lychbury were available on line and covered baptisms, marriages, deaths, tombstone inscriptions and various other details – some complete, some not. After scrolling through the lists I found her. There was her name and date of birth, November 27th, 1742.

'There's no record of her marriage, her death, or anything else,' I muttered, thinking her birthday wasn't far away. Maybe she'd left the village to live elsewhere though I had the idea that moving away from family and friends would have been unusual for a young girl in those days. But if she'd married someone from another parish, well – that could account for it.

With added curiosity I keyed in my own surname, Hadfield. There were a good few with that name in the area. The one that caught my attention was a Thomas Hadfield. He was born in Lychbury in 1738 and according to the records had departed for America in 1763, the year of Jane Lockhart's twenty-first birthday. I wondered what became of him. 'He must have known her,' I told myself. 'In a small place like this, he must have. And was he an ancestor of mine?' Inevitably, I wondered if they had been lovers. I unconsciously fished about the desk for my cigarettes then realised, as I'd done several times already since being there, that the house was strictly non-smoking.

***

A day later the mists returned; thicker this time and lower lying so that after dark a full moon was clearly visible. Shortly before eight I closed the computer and headed out into the cold night for something to eat at what by now was very much my local. With her image once again risen in my thoughts I decided to carry on by the Admiral Hawke, cross the road, light a cigarette and, torch in hand, visit the cemetery once more. The light was eerie, the place feeling even more cold and isolated from reality than it previously had, though the cigarette offered modest consolation. Her grave attracted me like an invisible beacon, morbid as that may seem. The first thing my torch picked out against the glistening wet slab were the flowers – fresh red carnations.

'This is bloody madness,' I breathed, leaning closer. Once more I heard her voice, soft as velvet, 'Jonathan.' But now there was no breeze to dispel the mist that closed about me.

'Who are you?' I whispered, letting drop the cigarette. 'Are you Jane Lockhart?'

I looked up and there was her face – but no, it couldn't be! It was the pattern of a human face formed by the twigs and branches of the tree above with the moon shining through. But it *was* the face of Jane Lockhart! I was convinced of it because her image I already knew. I could feel her presence. She was reaching out to me. I was frozen with more than just the cold - then I backed away, almost tripping over the stone edging of another grave. It's when you decide to run that fear really takes hold.

'Jonathan.' I heard it again but managed to quell a rising panic though my spine was pricking. Dreams are one thing; this was something else. Breathing long and hard, barely able to see through the fog, I made my way out of there, clanged shut the iron gate, looked over my shoulder and headed quickly as I could down the main street to the Admiral Hawke.

'Looks like you've seen a ghost,' quipped the barman as I dragged off my coat.

'Seen and bloody well heard!' I was tempted to exclaim, but instead I shrugged it off with a smile and a request for their evening menu. In the comforting warmth and sanity of the pub, amidst the mundane and worldly chatter and chink of glasses, I told myself I was still suffering from the traumas of earlier that year and that I needed to pull myself together. I determined I was going to get to the bottom of what was becoming - no, had become, an obsession causing hallucinations over someone long gone from this world. I poured my first glass of wine with a shaking hand.

***

'Jonathan.'

'What!' I turned away from the shop window and there she was, standing in bright sunlight with a dimpled smile on her face.

160

'Sorry If I scared you,' she said, touching my arm. But I wasn't scared at all. Not just then.

Her smile became a mild look of reproof when she added, 'You left me all alone the other day, Jonathan. Why did you do that?'

'I – I'm sorry. Something happened. Shall we walk for a while?' I took her hand. It was soft and warm as we strolled past half-timbered houses, mullioned windows and quaint old shops. The high street was moderately busy. As before, the village, the people, looked and felt as real as might be expected even though I had never been to Lychbury in the summer. As before I felt as if I – as if we, walked unseen and unheard by other people. She looked at me often with those wide eyes, smiling but saying nothing.

We'd strolled over an old stone bridge and stopped to peer down at the river when she squeezed my hand and said, 'Jonathan, let's cross over the road and walk back. We can go into the churchyard. We can sit a while and talk.' We carried on until reaching the gate, then as we entered the churchyard she said, 'Come along, now - let me show you something I know you would like to see.'

I followed as she stepped around the old gravestones. I knew where she was going. I knew I ought to be very afraid because something deep at the back of my mind kept on nagging, kept on telling me I should. Then she turned to place a hand on my cheek.

***

'Wakey-wakey, sir!' His voice crashed into my brain like gong. 'We close in five minutes.'

161

I blinked and stared about. For a second or two I didn't know where I was.

'You've 'ad a fair bit to drink,' said the publican. 'Just as well you aren't driving. Are you going to be all right walking home?'

'Y-yes,' I mumbled, struggling up and staring about the almost empty pub. 'Sorry, I didn't mean to cause embarrassment.' The wine bottle resting on my table was almost empty.

'No problem, but it's arctic out there and the fog's much thicker.'

Fastening my coat, I stumbled out through the door, shocked to full reality by freezing air. I lit another cigarette then hurried along the deserted road, looking straight ahead into grey obscurity, seeing no one, hearing myself mutter, 'Jesus Christ – what's happening to me?'

The street lamps, the houses about loomed vaguely from the fog, unreal, like phantom vessels appearing out of a dark sea. But the cold - that was all too real. I turned off the main road onto the unlit path leading to the house, the beam of my torch illuminating little more than a diffused, spectral glow in the mist close in front of me. Again I could hear her calling. The voice could have been nearby or only in my mind, if it was anywhere at all. I walked in fear of her image appearing out of that mist, not as the beautiful woman I had encountered in those dreams but as some ragged, red-eyed horror.

The voice only faded when I shoved my key into the front door lock. I slammed the door hard, checking twice that it was secured. Slipping off my coat and shoes in the so ordinary, so reasonable bright light of the hallway I asked myself again what was happening. Had I created a separate existence in my own mind when I conjured up the image of Jane Lockhart?

But those damned flowers were real enough. The flowers had to be the key. There had to be a perfectly logical explanation and I was to blame for creating something beyond reason, something out of practically nothing because of the state of my nerves. Someone from the village must be entering the cemetery at night and putting the flowers there.

I sat for a while with a glass of brandy, staring at some pointless television programme, knowing that before long I had to go to bed and sleep. I didn't want to do that. In front of the bathroom mirror I pondered on the fact that I was afraid when awake but not in the dreams. 'Shouldn't it be the other way around?' I asked, gazing at my own reflection.

***

I didn't dream that night, nor did I hear her voice. I would surely have remembered if I had. The day ought to have been relatively normal but I found some difficulty in concentrating on my work. The fog had not lifted entirely but at least there was a soft, pallid sun hanging low over the bare trees and village when I set out to grab some lunch.

I carried on past the Admiral Hawke then into the graveyard, thinking I'd be able to shake off whatever had taken a hold of me. There was a service of some kind going on in the old church. The organ was playing and the small group of people gathered in conversation by the porch served to dispel the mystery of the place. There was no voice, no image of Jane Lockhart - and the flowers were gone. Gone, yes - but something told me they would be there again sooner or later. So in the sanity and safety of those short daylight hours I was determined to knock this whole episode on the head.

I would return to the graveyard after dark.

***

I remained in the Admiral Hawke until after closing time and as so often I drank more than I ought; this time managing to stay awake. After leaving my laptop behind the bar I said my goodnights, stepped from that benign sanctum of light and comfort, crossed the road and walked along to the churchyard. It was bitter cold as ever and though the moon was still bright overhead, the mist had thickened considerably since my setting out earlier that evening. It enveloped the gravestones in an eerie haze that obscured anything beyond three or so metres.

As I approached the resting place of Jane Lockhart, I saw by moonlight there were as yet no carnations placed there. I had my cigarettes and I'd put on an extra layer of clothing. I would sit there all night if necessary to confront whoever was leaving flowers on that grave. I would make them tell me why they did it. But such logical reasoning did not prevent me being once more afraid.

There was an old wooden bench standing nearby, close enough to watch the grave without my presence being obvious. Expecting the seat would be damp I'd brought along a plastic bag to sit on. Once settled down I pulled out my cigarettes and lighter, then I hesitated: whoever came by might see the glow or smell the smoke. After a minute or so I decided to take a chance and light up. A cigarette or two would, or so I hoped, calm my nerves. My fingers were getting numb so I shoved them deep into my pockets, but at least the bench was comfortable and I was able to relax in body if not in mind. The night was profoundly quiet and still. The extra clothes were keeping me tolerably warm and after a while I felt somewhat easier over being there. I was so deep in thought that, after my first cigarette, the world beyond my immediate surroundings might no longer have existed.

***

She was laughing; her voice a soft chime on a warm, clear day. 'Jonathan, you left me again. How can we be together if you leave me? Now you have to stay, Jonathan. You have to stay.'

The sun was shining as she held my hand. We were standing at the cemetery gate. I had a vague impression of people on the opposite side of the road but there was no one close by.

'Something happened,' I replied. 'I didn't want to leave. I'm here with you now, Jane.'

'Yes, we are together now, Jonathan, as we should be. Shall we go on?'

'Yes, let's go on.'

She pushed open the gate and we stepped through. We made our way to the grave I knew so well. In summer sunlight it looked very different. But then it was different. The grave was empty. I gazed upon a deep hollow pit with earth piled either side, awaiting a body or bodies. There was no stone rising above it but the flowers were there, set aside and waiting.

'See,' she smiled, 'red carnations. I do so love red carnations, Jonathan - don't you?'

'Jane,' I answered. I didn't know what else to say. 'Jane,' I repeated. She smiled and began to lead me by the hand. She was irresistible.

The sun was waning. The pit was growing as we stood before it. Growing bigger and darker. Drawing me closer - ever closer. All I could see were her face and her eyes - eyes that grew larger and paler until there was nothing else in my beleaguered mind. Then I was drifting in utter blackness!

***

'Mr Hadfield, you're awake. That's good.'

His voice came out of darkness but the light was intensifying through my closed eyelids. I opened my eyes to find myself lying in bed, beneath warm blankets in a plain-walled room. I could make out some electronic gadgetry and an empty chair on one side and the dark-suited, bespectacled figure of a man standing over me on the other.

I stared about in total confusion before speaking. 'W-what's happened? Where am I?'

'You're in Macclesfield General Hospital recovering from hypothermia, Mr Hadfield. You are lucky to be alive.' I stared uncomprehending then he continued. 'You'd had rather a lot to drink. It seems you left the public house around midnight to sleep it off in the graveyard. Not at all sensible with the temperature below freezing if I may say so. Worse still, you had removed much of your clothing and lay sprawled across one of the old graves. A while longer and you would most likely have died. No real damage done, however.'

'How did I end up in here?' I asked.

'You were found by a group of yobbos – or should I say, youths, since one of them took it upon himself to report your situation to the emergency services on his mobile phone. Whatever they were up to there in the early hours of the morning we don't know since they cleared off without leaving a name.' The doctor looked at his watch then added, 'I must go now. The nurse will be with you shortly. You must remain here for the morning and try to rest.'

I remembered everything that had happened in that last dream, just as I had with the others. My mind was in turmoil - but I soon fell asleep again.

'Mr Hadfield!'

'God,' I groaned, seeing the nurse standing by the bed, 'how long have I been asleep this time?' Her face might have been chiselled out of granite.

'Almost four hours,' she snapped. 'If you will sit up I'll take your blood pressure then you'll be brought something to eat and drink. After that you should be fit enough to leave' As she fixed the sleeve around my upper arm she added, tersely, 'And we do not allow visitors to bring in flowers – though I'll overlook it as you are not staying.'

'Flowers?' I asked as she pumped up the sleeve, 'What flowers?'

She pointed toward the small table by the window. '*Those* flowers, Mr Hadfield.'

I turned aside to see laying there a bunch of red carnations. 'I've no idea who left those,' I mumbled. 'I'm renting a place in Lychbury. I don't know anyone there except the pub staff.'

167

'Well, Mr Hadfield,' declared the nurse, checking the blood pressure readout, 'she obviously knows you. No one saw her bring them in but the label says they're from someone called Jane. Oh, and your blood pressure is a little high but nothing to worry about.'

I sank back, murmuring, 'She was very lonely. She waited for me all those years.'

Turning to go the nurse said, 'Then I imagine she'll be out there waiting when you leave the hospital.'

Charabanc

She had been everything to him. Never a wrong word since they first came together. Never a misunderstanding. Not a trivial disagreement. In all the long years she'd done everything he could ask of her and more. Much more. They'd travelled good roads and bad, in sunshine and in rain – in the best and the worst of weather. They had seen all the sights anyone could wish to see and never a complaint, never a gripe. Who could say that about any woman? Who?

Now this. After all those fruitful years, it had come to this. The final act of their lives.

He wiped begrimed hands on the ragged cotton cloth, threw down the cigarette end, fingered a stubbled chin and stepped back, his task completed. She was ready, as once she'd always been ready. Proud and ready to go. Her chrome gleamed brighter than any royal tiara Alf could imagine. The big round headlamps, the bumpers, radiator grill - all of it. All of it polished and not a blemish to be seen. Not unless you knew where to look. And you'd need to look hard to find the odd trace of rust. There wasn't much. Not really.

And her coachwork! Oh, her coachwork! Poetry in rich maroon and mellow cream with little colour variations in places to give her extra character. Yes - polished and buffed to perfection. There had been some filling here and there over the years, what could anyone expect? Not even a Rolls Royce lasted forever. But who would know? Who? You couldn't tell by looking at the paintwork. Not the ordinary passer-by couldn't. You'd need to be an expert, more or less, to find anything about her like that.

His eyes feasted upon her sensuous lines. Upon curves that flowed as a creation inspired by nature. Like the form of a tendril or a reed in the breeze. Like the lines of a dolphin or the swooping flight of a bird. Here was a sublime work of automotive art. Here was a thing of beauty to be admired and cherished. And he had cherished her. Not the Venetian state barge, not the ceremonial coaches of the royals, not the altar of St. Peter's in Rome had enjoyed more care than he had lavished on old Daisy. That was why she looked the way she did today – proud, magnificent. And what if the suspension was down on one side? What if she did put out the occasional cloud of smoke? All right, perhaps more than occasional. It told of years of hard work, of honest work - no more and no less.

Yes, she was ready to emerge from the confines of the yard. Ready to set forth in splendour. She would progress along the main road to the admiring glances of all those fortunate enough to witness her passing. All those fortunate enough to see emblazoned along her sides in hand painted swirls of royal blue script, not flaking so much that you'd notice at first glance, *Skinner's Family Tours - Where the Sun Always Shines*.

Yes, her chrome sparkled. Yes, her coachwork glowed. And yes, she wasn't going anywhere at all! Never again.

Not officially at any rate.

Sighing as he trudged across the cobbled yard to the rear door of the house, Alf Skinner thrust his cloth into the pocket of sagging, once blue overalls, dirt and oil-patched now in the manner of a military camouflage. 'Time for a cuppa,' he muttered, rattling shut the warped wooden door that once had fitted the frame properly. 'Definitely time for a cuppa.'

Alf hovered by the speckled enamel gas cooker as the kettle began to boil, glanced at the large brown envelope that lay next to the potted plant on the table by the window. Having poured boiling water into a blue enamel mug that might have seen service in the trenches, having squeezed a reused tea bag hard against the side with tannin-blemished spoon, having ladled in two heaped white sugars and a dash of milk before briskly stirring the liquid, Alf stepped over to the table and sat down.

The envelope had been opened yesterday but its dismal contents, once revealed, had been replaced. Sipping from the mug, he had no intention of taking the papers out again. The message contained therein would be no different today than it had been when it first arrived. Over the last twenty-four hours, through the loneliness of the night, those terrible words had burned into his soul. '... *steering worn and in need of alignment ... front and rear tyres worn well beyond the legal limit ... brake pads to be replaced ... exhaust emissions unacceptable ... unable to consider renewal of your licence until ...*' Or words to that effect. And more.

'What the 'ell do they expect,' he breathed, brushing the envelope to the far edge of the table, 'bloody miracles? People don't want trips down the coast no more. Not the way they used to. What am I supposed to do? Change the bleedin' course of 'istory? Shove 'em on board at gunpoint?'

171

Alf lit a bent cigarette withdrawn from a crushed packet and, peering through time and tobacco yellowed net curtains he scrutinised the sky. There was broken cloud, moving slowly. From time to time a shaft of sunlight illuminated the coach.

Coach. There was a word to recall luxury and elegance. Coach. It once occupied the same genteel vocabulary, all but vanished from this accursed world of computers and mobile phones, as 'plush,' 'deluxe' and 'bespoke.'. Not that the people who once jostled and pushed aboard with grizzling children and overstuffed bags for a day out at the seaside, or their annual trip to the holiday camp, ever understood that. No - to them, to the crass and uncouth as well as to the innocent, Daisy was simply, 'The Sharra.'

In the old days she caused quite a stir when she appeared around the street corner like a blessing from heaven to stop at the appointed spot. Shouts of, 'Oi, it's the Sharra! The Sharra!' still rung in his ears. Eager faces beneath roller-curled or Brylcreemed hair would look up at him as they pressed to the edge of the kerb and the coach rattled to a stop. Rattled? Well, nearly everything on the road rattled in those days.

Anyway, once Daisy was on the open road, rattle or no, they'd start singing. No one was self-conscious. They just sang - just did it as though it was the most natural thing in the world. Well, they were happy in their own way. Happy to get away from the grind of everyday life. From skimping and saving. From routine, grey drudgery. Later on it was school trips or days out for the elderly - people who didn't, or couldn't, have a car of their own.

Then an incoming tide of sorrow. Regulations. Then more regulations.

Alf had ignored the regulations for some time but the regulations, or at least the faceless people who enforced the regulations, were not inclined to ignore him. And as with Canute, the king he'd been taught about at school on one of those few occasions when he felt the urge to take notice - there was no stopping the tide. There was no stopping it, that is, without the cash to undertake what the regulations demanded. He'd done what he could in his own workshop. He'd kept her on the road a fair while longer but it wasn't good enough for them and never would be. Now she stood waiting in the yard; a queen of the road, dethroned, sentenced to oblivion, condemned by the scribble of a nameless, uncaring bureaucrat. 'Some chinless bleedin' wonder,' muttered Alf.

Well his Daisy wouldn't be waiting much longer. Not for her the breaker's yard. She was setting out into the world this one last time. Setting out in pride and splendour with Alf's hands on the wheel, his feet treading the so familiar creaky pedals. Her greatest journey ever, that's what it was going to be, regulations or no. Her, and his, supreme sacrifice. Such a shame it had to be at night. The ignominy, the indignity of being stopped by the police hardly bore thinking about. But what a pity it had to be that way. What a pity she would not be seen in broad daylight, engine-revving - no, *proceeding* along the highway in chromed, painted and sign-written glory on that great and final day.

***

It was time. The yard doors stood wide open to the night but no one in the terraced houses opposite saw. No one cared. Television sets flickered ghost-light about the edges of closed curtains. Before him, the road beckoned.

The old engine protested much before coughing and wheezing to life, though he expected that. Now she turned over uneasily as though trying to recover her breath. After so many days standing idle, how could it be otherwise? But alive she was with every panel, bolt and fitting oscillating to her mechanical heartbeat. The gear lever trembled in anticipation of his touch. On the circular dial of the illuminated speedometer the hand quivered impatiently on six and a half miles per hour, though Daisy was yet to move. Well, *he* knew what it meant and that was all that mattered. The aroma of Bakelite, old leather and a lingering hint of stale tobacco sated his senses as might the rarest of exotic perfumes as she began to shudder forward.

She emerged through the doors, swaying onto the dimly lit road, a vessel about to embark upon forbidden waters, he let her wheeze to a halt then jerked back the handbrake. Through a crazed wing mirror Alf glanced at the open doors of the now vacant yard. 'Pah - why bother! Let 'em go inside an' nick the bleedin' lot. There's little enough left worth botherin' about. It's all here, Daisy. You and me. All here! An' don't we know the roads. When did we ever need all the fancy gadgets they go on about nowadays? Satnavs and whatever? Bollocks!'

Pushing the gear lever resolutely forward, he dropped the hand brake and let out the worn clutch pedal as his foot trod the loose play of the accelerator. The engine cleared its throat then roared like an angry bear. The coach lurched. Black smoke spluttered from the quivering pipe at her rear and she was on her way to the main road.

'Bollocks to the lot of 'em I say, Daisy! Bollocks!'

***

Mercifully, there were no complications. Daisy wheezed to a stop at numerous traffic lights, Alf peered out at brightly lit shops and passing people, held his breath when staring down at a police car at one busy junction. The hand of authority must be falling upon other victims for the world seemed content to ignore him altogether. Only on one occasion did his hand fall to the big metal button at the centre of the steering wheel to sound the horn, then he pushed it repeatedly. The sound rose and fell like the braying of a donkey, a sound that expressed real character.

Soon enough he had coaxed her away from busy traffic, from the glare of the inner suburbs and was passing through the green and manicured land of the well-to-do. Never for people here had been the likes of Daisy. They might have witnessed her passing in times gone by, if they'd bothered to look, for the route was a familiar and well-travelled one to Alf Skinner. Familiar indeed because it led to a once magic land. To the coast. To the seaside of bygone days. Most of the camps, the chalets and the caravan sites had gone but there was still a sweep of pebble beaches and the open sea. There were still the headlands and the high chalk cliffs.

The high chalk cliffs. Could there be a more fitting, a more dramatic end?

Suddenly he was afraid of what he had planned to do and the coach began to slow.

'What we needs is a bit of cheer!' rang his voice across empty seats of patched and faded cloth.

His hand darted to the glove compartment, invading the secret kingdom to close upon a small plastic case. No glance was needed to confirm it was what he sought.

'A good old sing-along is what we needs, Daisy! A good old sing-along!'

A click and the music began. Music they all used to love on those golden days out. Everyone knew the words by heart. Knew the words as if they had been born into the world singing them. On the first track of the tape was the song that had given its name to the one faithful love of his life. It began to play. The coach filled with life and laughter once more and they were singing, too. They were singing because they loved to sing and because they were leaving it all behind and going on the best and longest journey of their lives. And how could he not join in? Alf always joined in! 'Daiseee, Daiseee, give me your answer dooo ...!'

By the time the tape had reached, *The Sun Has Got His Hat On,* the road ahead was hemmed in by dark trees. It was a road little used by traffic at night because it led nowhere, though on a clear day there were good views along the coast and across to France from the headland. Soon the trees would shrink to bushes, the sky would open wide and the road ascend to pass through gorse and grassland. A coastguard observation hut had once stood at the very end of it - he remembered the hut from not so many years ago. One winter night a section of the cliffs had given way and it had fallen with part of the roadway to be shattered amongst the chaos of boulders below. He recalled peering nervously over the edge. It was so far down that any sign of wreckage was hard to make out and the boulders looked like small pebbles.

Alf turned up the sound and called at the top of his voice, 'Is everybody happy?'

The coach rang with memories. They replied as one, 'Yeah - yeah - yeah!'

Less than a mile to go; a mile because Daisy had no time for kilometres. Only a few more bends in the road and there would be only the night sky ahead. The night sky and the stars. He imagined her - imagined the two of them sailing into the sky and up toward those bright stars. A silhouette drifting in majesty across the face of a full moon. His favourite tune playing. Immortalised.

On the road ahead flashed a blue light.

'Gawd 'elp us,' he breathed, switching off the tape player. 'Can't be! Bleedin' police 'ere of all places. Bleedin' police!'

A glint of metal caught in the headlamps. The coach slowed.

Something lay part blocking the road. Something large, smooth and silver that defied description. Without a shade of doubt it was not a police car.

'Stone me - what the 'ell's this! One of them new leisure centres? No, can't be. Not stuck right across the road.'

The coach, engine revving, shivered to a standstill little over her own length from the obstruction - a sight that struck him as ever more bizarre as he peered out. Of the blue light, there was no longer any sign. Alf wrenched the handbrake up, slipped the gears into neutral and, half rising from the seat, leaned to stare harder through the windscreen. Whatever the object was, part of it, maybe most of it, was hidden by darkness and bushes. For long seconds he remained staring. 'Why the 'ell would anyone leave a thing like that up 'ere. Now what, Daisy? Now what? No other road for us to take an' we can't get by it. Gawd 'elp us, old girl! Gawd 'elp us!'

The blue light reappeared, this time much brighter. Alf's eyebrows twitched. A door! There was a door opening in the side of - of - whatever it was. Figures appeared, scurrying silhouettes. Five - no, six - maybe seven. Suddenly they were in his headlights and moving toward the coach. Alf Skinner fell back into the seat, hands pressed to his face. 'Oh, Gawd, no! Not bleedin' little green men! Gawd 'elp me, no! I can't take none of this! Oh, Gawd! Oh, Gawd!'

In moments they had reached the front of the coach and, heads bobbing up and down, passed from the yellow glare of the headlamps. His hands fell to the steering wheel. He took a deep breath and, very, very slowly, turned to look.

They were there. He could see them clearly. They were staring at him. They were gathered about the passengers' door. Waiting.

Alf leaned across, gazed through the window, his breath forming a patch of condensation on cool glass. Seven pairs of eyes peered up into his. Large eyes. Deep eyes. Eyes without pupils or eyelids.

'I'm bleedin' dead already,' he groaned, slumping back into the driver's seat. 'That's it. We went and done it, didn' we, Daisy, old girl. Went over the bleedin' edge and now I'm dead an' we've ended up in a world of bleedin' freaks!'

'Excuse us,' chirped the voice from within his head.

'Yes, excuse us,' rippled others in its wake.

Alf looked aside once more. They were still there in the darkness. Not only there but pressing closer about the door. Alf squirmed in his seat. Alf hoped the door was locked.

'Excuse us,' came the voice again, followed by a chorus of, 'Yes, excuse us, won't you.'

This was no time to panic. Or was it? Easing himself across to the door, he once more stared down at them, a finger wagging dismissal, his nose touching the glass. 'Look 'ere now - now, piss off you 'orrible little bleeders! I don't want no funny business! Just leave me alone and clear off out of it!'

His remonstrations had no effect. He perceived not the slightest reaction among them. Grasping the handle, he cranked down the window with a determination he hoped would bring about their retreat if not total disappearance, and thrust out his face. 'Now look 'ere! Just piss off! Just - just scarper! Savvy? Comprendi?'

'We require your assistance for an important task,' chirped the voice within his skull. 'Yes, a very important task,' chimed in the rest.'

Which of them had originated the statement he was unable to determine. None of the creatures appeared to possess a mouth.

For a time he remained speechless, then - 'What! You want *me* to 'elp *you* out? Me!'

'That is correct,' came the reply.

'Yes, absolutely correct,' came the follow-up.

'Bloody 'ell! Me? Why me? I don't want to get mixed up in no funny business - 'specially now I've gone bleedin' mad?'

'You have nothing to lose,' came the voice, 'you were about to destroy yourself. We sensed it before you arrived.'

'Yes, destroy yourself,' echoed the rest. 'Now there is no need.'

''Ow the 'ell did you know what I -' muttered Alf, weakly. 'An' - an' what d'you mean, there's no need?'

'No need,' repeated the first voice.

'None at all,' confirmed the rest.

Alf returned to his seat and gazed at the silver form still obstructing the road ahead. Still part illuminated by his wavering headlights. He was aware once more of the engine running. Its uneven rattle, its rise and fall strangely reassuring. Perhaps in a moment, perhaps if he stared ahead at the night sky a while longer, the odd, worrisome creatures gathered by the coach would vanish and the world would revert to normality. Whatever normality was.

Alf looked aside once more. They were still there.

Again the voice. 'Your vehicle is ideal for our needs. We wish to hire it.'

'Yes, we're quite willing to hire it,' agreed the others. 'We understand that is what you do.'

'Hire it? Hire Daisy?' he croaked in disbelief. 'What - I mean - why d'you -?'

'We have encountered an anomaly with our field-phase synchronisation and polarity interface,' came the voice.

'We have broken down,' followed the rest.

'Very well, broken down,' continued the voice. 'We are the first colonists. We and the ones who landed elsewhere today. They are waiting for us to join them but we are unable to communicate.'

'Cannot communicate,' came the now anticipated follow-up, 'but we really do have to join them.'

'If we cannot join them in time,' continued the first, 'our operation to acquire this world for ourselves may fail.'

'May fail entirely,' added the others.

Alf's face reappeared at the window. His entire head emerged into the chill night air. His neck prickled as if in anticipation of the guillotine's blade. He noted their height - less than that of an average human. He observed beads of moisture on reptilian skin. 'You mean you little green blee -, you mean you lot are takin' the country over? The government? The department of transport, even?'

'The entire planet. Everything.'

'Everything,' agreed the rest.

He stared down, looked at each in turn then asked, 'And, er, what do I get out of all this? Why the 'ell should I bother to 'elp you lot out? Tell me that.'

'We will reward you for your help,' came the voice.

'Yes, a splendid reward,' confirmed its companions.

Alf's head protruded even further as he eyed the creature closest. The rest shuffled about in anticipation. For no other reason than its proximity, he had decided that the nearest individual was the representative of the party. 'And, er - this reward - what sort of reward do we 'ave in mind, like? Cash, maybe? I mean, *real* cash? And tax free, mind you!'

'Anything within our power to give,' came the voice, 'but money will soon be useless. We must hurry. And there are more of us.'

'It is most important that we hurry,' chirped the rest.

Alf glanced through the night at the silver object, then back. 'Reward, eh. Anything I want is it? Right - 'op in! She'll seat twenty-eight with five standing.' Already he was releasing the passenger door. 'An' no monkey business or I stop the coach an' we don't go nowhere - agreed?'

As he finished speaking, the blue light flickered. A stream of figures emerged from the door of the object, bobbing, scurrying behind the bushes, into the light of his headlamps and toward the coach. He did not watch them clamber awkwardly aboard, did not count their number, but stared out at the sky, feeling the coach rock gently and hearing the creak of her suspension.

The door slammed shut.

Alf pushed the gear lever into reverse and glanced into the mirror. A sea of blank faces stared back at him. 'Now, 'old tight while I turn the old girl about. It'll take a few minutes. We'll discuss terms, all proper, like, then we're on our way!'

***

It was morning and the sun hovered in a cloudless sky. From time to time he observed shoals of them at high altitude - silver disks in some kind of formation sweeping at extreme speed from horizon to horizon. A few hours back, before daylight, there had been the odd rumble - explosions he presumed, and frequent glares had lit up the sky. To the east a dark pall of smoke hung over the town. His town.

Ahead, the road was clear. Not just clear but devoid of moving traffic, though here and there lay abandoned the occasional car or truck.

'Never seen it like this before, old girl. Never.' he smiled, listening to the purr of the engine - Daisy's brand new engine. 'Marvellous ain't it - bleedin' marvellous! Won't need no more petrol, ever, won't need no more oil, an' no more worry about worn tyres!' He reached into the glove compartment to touch the brown envelope that only yesterday had lain threateningly on his table by the window. 'Who'd have thought we'd be out an' about on the road again like this an' not a bleedin' copper in sight. Who'd 'ave thought it, eh, old girl? You're queen of the road again, Daisy! You're the star! An' we got one of them fancy satellite navigational machines. All I 'ave to do is say where we want to go an' she'll tell us. Bleedin' marvellous!'

Alf glanced at the mirror. At the seats, at the empty road behind, then back to the seats. The seats were no longer empty. Each was occupied by a

183

silent, unblinking figure. Each figure wore smart office attire, each was groomed and manicured to perfection. Some still clutched briefcase or shoulder bag, some a black, rolled umbrella. In the seat directly behind the driver, in frozen limbo, sat one with short black hair, horn-rimmed spectacles and neatly trimmed moustache. In his hands a file titled, *Driver and Vehicle Licensing Authority.*

'Are we all sittin' tight for a day of delight?' peeled out Alf Skinner's voice. 'Are we all ready for a song – for a good old tra-la-la?'

His finger alighted upon the newly installed dashboard console. The passengers stirred and blinked. Cleared their throats and smiled in vacant, pre-programmed contentment.

'Right then, 'ere we go!'

Her engine purred. In clear morning light the coach progressed, immaculate. Sun flared from polished chrome, glowed upon rich maroon and cream bodywork, spotless smooth, that displayed afresh, *Skinner's Family Tours - Where the Sun Always Shines.* From Daisy's innards arose a chorus of voices. A chorus in harmonious and blissful union. Alf glanced again at the mirror and smiled. Never had, *Land of Hope and Glory*, sounded so sweet to his ears.

Daisy followed the curves of the road, the gentle rise and fall of summer hills. A beetle-bright splash of colour moving in a placid, deserted landscape.

Journey

The room was burdened with age. It was heavy with a biding stillness. It would have seemed quiet upon first entering. Quiet as you moved toward the gaping, toothless mouth of the brick-arched fireplace about which the chairs and table were arranged. Quiet unless you listened to the remorseless tick of the ebony-cased mantle clock where insect antenna hands quivered over black spider numerals. Quiet until you became aware of a rapid clicking like the frenzied dance of dried bones.

A newspaper moved. Whispered as a starched shroud.

Someone coughed a hard, staccato cough. An anvil blow inside a stone chapel.

The clicking stopped. Silence welled as an angry sea. Two faces raised from their own shadows. Faces hanging as crumpled parchment that passing years had penned to the limit. Pale eyes whose pools of memory were too deep and dark for their possessors to fathom. The newspaper trembled, billowed, disturbed the air about it. It was a movement that signalled, 'Be quiet! Don't cough again!'

The clicking resumed.

Then an outrage. That same person cleared her throat and coughed a second time.

The newspaper quivered. Mantis arms lowered. Eyes blinked, magnified large behind scratched spectacle glass. The clicking stopped again. Crow fingers held needles poised. Crow face raised up. Dull-bead eyes peered from behind fragile

185

spectacles toward the alcove by the fireplace. The throat cleared again and her eyes, grey, rock-pool creatures, regarded them in turn. Now she spoke: grating brick upon brick. 'Is it tea time yet? Does anybody know?'

The form that had mustered the words stirred and though the room was moderately warm, it reposed beneath the tumulus of a heavy grey coat. A coat harbouring within its depths countless flakes, crumbs, fragmented bus tickets and a decaying purse. No one had ever seen Mrs Owens downstairs without the grey coat. No one cared to.

Nor had anyone who used the room ever suggested Mrs Owens resembled a toad. At least not whilst she was present. Eyelids sliding, mouth chewing - always, she was chewing. When she was close by, they could hear her jaws at work. Mrs Owens sometimes fell asleep. Then her snores rose and fell like the whirring of an old sewing machine. Louder even than the snores of Mr Parsons when he drifted across that uncertain threshold. The Mr Parsons who, presently awake, glinted horn-rimmed light from above the sagging newspaper.

'Eh, what? Tea?' squeaked Mr Parsons. A protesting, rusted gate. 'Did you say tea? Tea shouldn't be long now, Martha, eh. Shouldn't be long.'

Crow fingers set pale blue knitting down upon the nearest chair. The vacant chair. Mr Geddis' chair. The voice grated into something akin to life. 'It is time for tea. Yes, it is time for tea.'

'Always late,' chewed the toad.

'Always has been,' rasped the crow. Eyes turned to the circular table standing as a focal point of emptiness - a small, dark-lacquered table with cream lace cloth. The carpet on which the table stood bore autumn leaf pattern on a background of earthen brown that served, almost, to conceal the evidence of spills.

The surge had passed. Crow fingers wavered then descended upon wisps of knitting. The newspaper raised high to obscure its owner. Once more the room was quiet.

Except, of course, for the spiteful clock, the chewing and click-click-click of needles.

Somewhere in the house a door slammed. A distant voice sounded. A rattle. The scuffing of a trolley in the hallway outside. A sigh of air as the door swung open, then the girl entered. 'Here we all are,' she smiled. 'Tea and our favourite biscuits!'

The mantis and the crow iron-pump wheezed and prised themselves more or less upright. The toad continued chewing. From beneath the coat, a subterranean growl. On the table was placed the tray with fluted china teapot, four delicate, matching cups and saucers, and the milk jug - all displaying gold tendrils and pastel-mauve flowers. From a gaudy tin box the girl laid out a neat array of rectangular, scalloped biscuits. Glancing at the empty chair, she asked, 'Has anyone seen Mr Geddis? He's not in his room or in the TV lounge.'

An instantaneous response to the question would have surprised her. She knew they disapproved of her even more than they disapproved of Mr Geddis. Under the open house coat her blouse was cut too low, her skirt too short, her hazel eyes too bright, her light chestnut hair too long. She bore the guilt of youth and of hope. Worse, she showed no remorse.

'Takes himself out for a stroll, sometimes,' clicked the mantis, eyes averted.

Pouring tea into three of the four cups, the girl glanced up. Through the curtains, through leaded casement window she saw him. On the path that led by the house, through the gardens and down to the stream, a stooped figure made its way, swaying from side to side as though treading the deck of a small boat in a lapping sea. With each step his hand reached out to grip the top of a rustic fence that ran by the side of the path.

'Ee'll be off somewhere this time of the day,' chewed the toad.

'She's still new,' chided the mantis. 'Didn't know, eh - didn't know! You'll have to learn. They all 'ad to learn.'

Their eyes turned upon her as one and they smiled blank smiles. She was still afraid, even after several weeks at the house. The girl straightened up. A butterfly fresh from the sun. Ill at ease and feeling she had strayed into a mouldering catacomb.

***

Mr Geddis slowed, rested, felt his heart pound as the thudding of distant hooves. His hand fell upon the timber fence to steady an uncertain balance. Ahead, the overgrown path descended gently toward the stream under a hazed November sky. A tang of damp leaves pervaded the cool air. Why go this way at all? Why go on when all that was left was to go back as he always must? Go on today. Go back today. Go on tomorrow. Go back tomorrow. A pendulum set in motion by mindless force. Impetus behind a train of gears that in turn drove a monstrous clock-hand on an endless, repetitive course. Its purpose quite forgotten.

And yet. And yet -.

Long ago he had known other paths, other roads, other skies. He recalled images of a bigger world, golden bright, with more paths, more roads than anyone could ever hope to follow. Now there was only one. It went nowhere, yet it might go everywhere. And it led away from the house. A house where even his memories would perish if he did not carry them into daylight now and again.

The path turned when it reached the stream and there it ended at the old wooden seat. He had never gone beyond the seat. Mr Geddis hobbled on. It was pleasant by the stream because the stream was life and on its journey it cared nothing for the house. Where the stream came from he did not know, but it was free as he once had been, rushing on into another time, another place. And the seat. The seat was part decayed. Once, like the house, it had been fresh and new in the summer sun. Now it stood alone by the stream. Forgotten.

***

The horseman, lean and bright-eyed, reined back, bringing the dappled grey mare to a halt. Her nostrils flared, her hooves struck wet shingle. Ever alert, he looked back the way he had ridden, a hand raised to shield his eyes against a part-risen sun that glared over the horizon as a reptile eye. The barren landscape lay still and silent. A landscape scoured by time. Wasted hills and mesas misted pale against a featureless sky. A world of hidden menace.

189

He had to go on. Something baleful had arisen to move unseen within that bleak realm. On the air was the breath of a fearful beast. Something that stalked, drew close and would reach out to him with evil touch. Against it the bright sword at his side and the courage in his heart would be of no avail. He had never beheld that dark form, yet it was familiar. Perhaps it had always been there, worming unseen through time. Perhaps he had always known it would one day seek him out.

Before him swept the river, narrowing, quickening on its journey into the sombre gorge he was about to enter. Glancing back for the last time, he lashed with the rope and called out to have his call return in mocking echo from the gorge that lay ahead. The mare shook her main, stamped and started forward. Before the horseman arose dark walls that overhung the narrow gravel margins of a river bereft of life. It might lead to oblivion yet he must go where the beast could never follow.

***

The girl lifted a number of small, labelled boxes from the pocket of her housecoat. 'Time for our pills,' she said, her face an off-the-shelf, a regulation smile as she looked down at the name printed on each label. 'Now, let's see who takes what, shall we?'

'Have it too easy nowadays, all of 'em,' chewed the toad from her dim alcove.

The mantis cleared his throat as though about to agree but began to cough. A decrepit car refusing to fire, he rocked, shaking back and forth in the chair. The crow eyed him open mouthed, squinted at the girl, as if to say, 'See! See what you've done!'

'Too easy,' muttered the toad as the coughing subsided.

The girl, frozen in the act of administering their pills, continued her dispensation.

'Miss Mountsey,' she said, placing two pink capsules, a blue and a white pill on that part of the table closest to the crow, 'and Mr Parsons. Only these blue ones for you today.'

She glanced at the grey bulk in the alcove. 'Mrs Owens, dear, I'll put yours down here by the tea pot.' She had no intention of approaching the toad. No wish for entrapment within the invisible ectoplasm of old rugs tinged with ammonia that surrounded Mrs Owens. Ectoplasm, she thought, was not a bad analogy. Mrs Owens had been, so others said, a spiritualist and clairvoyant. What she saw, what she might claim to have seen was of no concern to the girl. The toad continued to chew. Then a dry-leaf rustle as the mantis reached for a pill next to his teacup. The crow rocked, shuddered forward, white talons outstretched.

The girl stepped back, her skin alive with the touch of imaginary insects. She fancied the two might leap out of their chairs and seize her in skeletal grip. Seize and hold her down whilst the toad arose to fall upon and engulf her in fetid blackness. Too close, she felt herself in danger of contamination through their malaise.

'Well, I'd better go and find Mr Geddis, hadn't I,' she said, returning the little boxes to the sanctuary of her coat pocket.

'Oooh, going to find Mr Geddis,' cackled the crow.

'Not 'ere,' grated the mantis. 'He's gone out.'

'Too good for us,' muttered the toad. Her comment was followed by a low, wheezing growl and a belch in whose aftermath, but only for brief moments, she ceased chewing.

The girl fingered a wisp of hair from above her eyes and retreated to the door. Mr Geddis was next. She liked Mr Geddis. He was old as the rest but not old the way they were old. They inhabited a world of decay - a world of furtive scampering, of dusty wings fluttering in some dark, obscure vault. Not Mr Geddis. Within Mr Geddis, within the layered windings of all those years, a light shone. A flame that defied smoke-laden glass.

***

Mr Geddis halted where the fence ended. Long ago it must have gone all the way down to the stream, but not now. Here and there, nestled amidst long grass, were the decayed stumps of vanished posts. People from the house, people of his age, were not supposed to go as far as the stream. They had told him he shouldn't. Often they had.

He gripped the knurled walking stick, tested it against soft ground whilst his free hand fell upon the sagging pocket of his tweed jacket, a jacket that denied the possibility of its having once been smart and new. For a fourth or fifth time he touched the pocket, reassuring himself that it contained what it had always contained; the chipped, cherrywood pipe and battered old tin that held his precious tobacco. The very fabric of the coat exuded the aroma tobacco. A comforting aroma to Mr Geddis. A stink to Mrs Owens and to Miss Mountsey. He'd heard them mutter about it as he passed through that room. It made Mr Parsons cough, so they said. But

Mr Geddis knew Mr Parsons wanted it to appear as though it made him cough so others would sympathise.

Once seated by the stream, Mr Geddis would press loose tobacco into the charred bowl of the pipe. He would light it with a match, draw upon the bitten stem in an ecstasy of satisfaction none of them could begin to understand, then exhale volumes of lazy smoke in grateful culmination of that simple act.

Furrow-faced Dr Sutcliffe did not approve, either. From under heavy eyebrows he would announce, 'You really must give up that filthy habit, Mr Geddis - for your own sake as well as for the sake of others!'

Nurse Kenning, no doubt giving out the pills and wondering where he had got to - would smile and say quietly, 'I'm supposed to take those away from you, Mr Geddis. Now try not to let them see you smoking or you'll get me into trouble.'

He had known a girl like her a long time ago. She had shining chestnut hair and hazel eyes and she laughed like Nurse Kenning. Such a long time ago. Once more his hand fell to the pocket and he trod slowly on.

***

Beneath an overhanging precipice, the dappled mare slowed. There was no longer room to remain on the gravel unless the horseman dismounted and led her. He did not care to do that. The gorge had narrowed to a grim chasm, the river now a raucous torrent, though the water was not too deep close by the edge and, with care, they could enter a short way. But only a short way. What the river seized in its anger, it would never set free.

The rock walls here were so high as to all but banish morning light. Further and the river churned in terrifying disorder, roaring, leaping over shattered boulders whilst the chasm taunted with subterranean growl. He could not see what lay ahead but whatever danger might threaten, he would not, could not turn back. A snort - the dappled mare let back her ears and shook her mane, afraid to go on. Leaning forward, the horseman spoke. Above the tumult she heard his call. 'Go, my beauty! Go!'

They pushed on beneath drizzled walls whose chill breath drew away their warmth and made the horseman shiver. Bellowing chaos, the river contrived to drag them into its midst. Cold spray lashed. Mortal fear bestrode their path. But when his spirits were at their lowest, when the horseman imagined this fearful place would never release them, he perceived the chasm beginning to widen. The dappled mare struggled on and as she did so, the river slowed and was less turbulent. The cliff walls, so oppressing, began to recede, to diminish in height. Further ahead, the gorge turned, lightened, opened to a valley, speckled here and there with colour. The horse was guided clear of the river so that her hooves crunched wet gravel, then he urged her on until at last a newly risen sun danced bright on the water and they were bathed in glorious warmth. On they went, the mare's pace quickening. The river continued wider until, in the distance, it spread across the horizon. At its far side the horseman saw low, green hills. Very soon, they must reach shallow water. The dappled mare sensed his feelings and started forward as though their journey had only just begun.

***

From their half-light world they watched her set out along the path. Watched through starched net curtains as the girl hurried on to disappear behind the leafless trees backing onto the garden.

'That'll be *his* pills,' grated the mantis, shaking his disgruntled newspaper then raising it as if to say he didn't care now and never had cared.

Plastic needles clicked. 'He's got *her* running about all right,' squeaked the crow.

'Hand me, fetch me, carry me,' chewed the toad. 'Hand me, fetch me, carry me.'

Plastic needles clicked quicker. Clicked furiously. Their sound filled the room. A frantic tapping of blind creatures in some forgotten, buried chamber. The toad moved. Leaned, wheezed, and still chewing, placed her china plate upon the table. On the plate lay broken, half eaten biscuits. A microcosm of eroded escarpments, plateaus and mesas in a ceramic desert. About them stood the china teacups, each a towering cenotaph. And beyond, set within the vast cosmos of the room, a monstrous, morbid trinity of dissolution.

***

Reaching the end of the fence, the girl stopped where Mr Geddis had stopped. The stream was not far away and Mr Geddis would be waiting. She had been there often before to find him. Sometimes they would sit and talk or she would simply listen. Often he would point out things she would have passed by without seeing. Rare plants clustered on the bank by the water. A bird resting in a nearby tree, gathering

195

strength to make the journey to some warmer, faraway place where, perhaps, Mr Geddis himself had once set youthful foot.

At the stream she turned then followed the narrow, grassy path where it curved around to the old bench. And there was Mr Geddis sitting in pale sunlight.

Nurse Kenning smiled, moved closer. 'Mr Geddis! Mr Geddis – I -.' She stopped, leaned closer, reached out a trembling hand. 'Oh - Mr Geddis!'

His eyes were closed. By his side on the wooden seat lay the cherry wood pipe and unopened tobacco tin. She stooped over his silent form, aware of the busy stream rushing by, murmuring over the rocks with a beat of muffled hooves. The knurled walking stick had fallen from his grip and lay on the bank where its tip bobbed in the water. She laid a hand on his shoulder. Breathed the incense tang of tobacco. 'Mr Geddis - not you. Please, Mr Geddis, not you. Anyone but you.'

His hand was already cold to her touch. Cold and rough as ancient wood.

The girl knelt down, began to cry. Tears shone on her cheek as the clear waters of a distant river touched by sunlight.

***

The river was wide, braided where smooth sandbanks lay exposed beneath a blue sky. Forward they went, the horse shedding sapphire clouds as she pounded through the shallows. The horseman saw where hills divided to form a fertile valley and closer, on the riverbank, where people gathered.

One of them watched him approach, a shimmering image rising as yet indistinct from the water.

He reined in the mare and lifted a hand to shade his eyes. Yes, it was her! He knew it was her! Now closer, he recognised the smiling face, bright hazel eyes and pale chestnut hair. She moved to the water's edge, hurried barefoot into the shallows and raised an arm. The horseman called her name. Called out and laughed. Laughed louder than the waters of the river. She was waiting. Now was the time. Now!

The dappled mare plunged forward. Thundered as his heartbeat over the shallows in a cascade of myriad suns. His laughter coursed ahead as they bounded on and the girl's laughter sped as a bird to join it. Their voices circled, swooped, danced together as the new day began.

Full length novels by this author

The Devil in Eden
The Man Who Sought Eternity
Return of The Hero
Shadow of The Beast
The Singing Stones

Further works by Jeff Clarke may be found on

www.jeffreypeterclarke.co.uk

And on his author page at:
https://fiction4all.com/ebooks/a1549.htm